AFTER

BONDAGE

AND

WAR

AN HISTORIC FICTIONAL NOVEL

DAVID CLAIRE JENNINGS

After Bondage and War

Downtown Books Publishing, Auburn, NY

ISBN-13: 978-0-6924-6658-2
ISBN-10: 0692466584

For those who have inspired, cared and helped-
Abraham, Jimmy, Nick and Joan

Foreword

Slavery was a stain on our country. It deeply falsified our founding ideals and was a longstanding shame for us in the eyes of the world. In the first hundred years of our history, we developed as two divergent societies and cultures based on two different visions in interpreting our founding ideals. Adams had a vision for a country of enterprising merchants and property owners with emerging industrialism in small towns and cities bound together under a central government - a system of Federalism. Jefferson had a vision of an agrarian society of independent small farmers with slavery under more localized governance in states. The North and South grew apart.

The period of the Civil War and its aftermath of failed Reconstruction was a watershed moment in our history, and perhaps its most important moment. As the regional and sectional issues heated up beyond reconciliation, the country blew up. The Union was preserved and slavery was abolished. But the South was devastated and the country's wounds have never completely healed.

What if the Civil War had not been fought? Would slavery have ended a couple decades later as the rest of the country industrialized? What would have happened if Lincoln had not been assassinated? Would the subsequent century of racism and sectional divide have been lessened? What would have happened if Eli Whitney, or anyone else, had not invented the cotton gin, or the boll weevil had been successful, or the world market for cotton as a raw material had declined 50 years earlier than the early 20th century?

While the backdrop for the story covers a century of our history, beginning with the antebellum period, progressing through parts of the Civil War and failed Reconstruction, and ending around 1900, the characters resonate with thoughts and feelings we all share today: frustration, hopelessness, loneliness, spiritual longing, friendship, and love. Like all of us, there are parts of our being that we can define as evil, or morally corrupt, and parts that are pure and good. As Shakespeare once said, "There is nothing either good or bad, but thinking makes it so." In addition, as peoples' lives progress with time, the fundamental nature of their character may change. We readers may start out rooting for one person that we believe to be a morally good person, and end up feeling that he or she has fallen short or utterly failed in his or her growth, or even has become corrupt and evil.

As I have come to re-know David after more than forty years apart, I have learned that he cares about and feels these things deeply. Through his extensive study, reading, and writing, he has developed a great sensitivity for our history and country and has gravitated toward a care and concern for its South.

I was the consummate Yankee, having been raised outside of New York City and having lived 10 years in Upstate New York, who knew nothing about the South. However, for the past 44 years I have lived in Georgia or Alabama. From metropolitan Atlanta to the most rural area of northern Alabama, I have come to know and understand the South as it has become. The New South rose from her ashes when she was rebuilt after the war. The South began to industrialize. For the rural Deep South however, much remains the same as it was in the past. Many of the positive characteristics of the southern culture embodied in this book are alive and well today, particularly in the rural areas. A deep abiding faith in the love of God, family and country still prevail in most of the people I know. And for many southerners, the Civil War continues to be a deep wound in their hearts.

The people of the South that I have come to know over the years are steadfast in their views and willing to lend a hand to anyone needing help, be it friend or stranger.

I am an educator by calling and a story teller by nature and David is a feeling historian. Several months ago, David asked me if I would read the book he was writing as a favor. It only took one reading for me to become intrigued by the characters and their story. Since then our old friendship has come alive in a new way, now that we are much older and have lived our lives and careers. Though thousand of miles apart, we have mentored each other and labored together to produce this book. With our care and concern for all the American people, we believe *After Bondage and War* to be a sensitive and important statement about this period of history and the people who lived through it.

Not since Stephen Crane's *Red Badge of Courage*, has this story been told with such emotional intensity and pathos. I feel we have treated it with a broader reach, dimension and poignancy. Through its personal recounting of history and its very human characters, it is our intention that our readers will feel this way also.

We hope so and hope you enjoy the story.

- Joan Austin

Contents

Prologue

The old man paused in his daily walk to rest on his favorite bench on the quad of the Miami of Ohio campus. He enjoyed the energy of the young students, their passion for civil rights and to end an unjust war. It was the 1960's.

He told them about his grandfather and his struggle 100 years ago. He told them about the Civil War and his grandfather's friend David whose name had been chosen for his father. He wanted them to gain a perspective that can only come from knowledge of the past.

————————◦————————

Josiah was tired, not in his muscles or bones from a hard day's work, in his soul for the loss he had suffered and the apprehension of what was to come. He slowly walked down the hard-packed and rutted red clay dirt road leading away from the Savannah Oaks plantation. He felt old beyond his years, and the simmering sultry heat and humidity of the southern Mississippi summer added to his fatigue the longer he walked. The massive live oaks, with their curtains of hanging Spanish moss provided some shade, but held the humidity so close to the ground that he could feel the droplets of water floating in the air around him.

He remembered the last time he had traveled this road, as a young man 13 years ago, when he was brought to Savannah Oaks. This time the journey was for a different purpose and under different circumstance.

Now he was traveling away from the place - his forced home for those last arduous, grueling and cruel years. The farther he walked, the further he remembered that bitter past journey on this road from Natchez. His thoughts drifted back to that

1

earlier time, to his brief happiness with Josena and his accomplishments then.

The live oaks with the hanging moss became less oppressive and brought him a sense of calmness and peace he had not felt earlier. Hope began to fill his heart. Now he would have the chance to find his beloved Josena. He began to walk faster.

This long day had begun with the arrival of the federal authorities at Savannah Oaks. They had come to broker the release of the plantation's slaves. Although the war had officially ended in April when Lee surrendered at Appomattox, the fighting didn't stop immediately, but continued in the western sections of the country.

The South had been so completely devastated and crippled by the war, communication was almost non-existent with virtually no functioning telegraph service. While communication in southern cities had been difficult, the southern plantations, which had always been spread far and wide in the Deep South, were more isolated than ever. It had taken from April until July for federal authorities to finally arrive at Savannah Oaks.

With the arrival of the government people, the plantation's slaves were gathered together. Some came from the fields, some from their cabins, the rest from the mansion. They assembled in the big yard in the front of the main house. They stood in groups and alone, anticipating a change but not knowing what it would mean. Some of them stood near the pole where they had been bound and lashed on so many occasions.

The government men explained to them that they were freed. This pronouncement was unprecedented, unfamiliar, but joyously welcome for the human beings who had always been enslaved, always been the property of some other human being, in one place or another. The authorities explained that there was hope for government programs to help them. They assured the emancipated people that the Freedmen's Bureau would make its best effort, with limited funding and political support, to provide for them.

The ideas they were considering were for better education, land provision, legal rights, and a societal readjustment to a free labor agricultural system. These noble plans for reconstruction had not been worked out and could not be guaranteed. A free labor system was a concept the South had no experience with or knowledge about. The many governments involved would debate and contend for authority.

But on this day, their message was received as both hopeful and frightening for the former slaves who were just now released. In the end, the politicians in the South and Washington looked out for their own interests and little was done to help them, despite the best intentions of the Freedmen's Bureau and some in the government.

As the former slaves stood there not quite knowing what would come next, they were told that for now they could leave as they wished and go where they wished. The younger ones were anxious to go and face a new future. The older ones were hesitant to leave their familiar life and more frightened of the unknown. None of their ancestors had traversed this free world before them.

They must be on their own and care for themselves. Their security and sustenance would be their own. There was no place to live, no food to eat. No one would provide. This was the end of a co-dependent society, a cruel security, where some would be forced to work for others and the others would provide for their care. The enslaved and the enslavers would part their ways.

They could search for their families, travel freely throughout the country and contract for their labor as best they could arrange. For the first time in their lives, those gathered in front of the main house realized that they owned their own selves.

This was both an exhilarating and worrisome revelation, for they were homeless now, they had nowhere to go, and their life was going to become very difficult in new and unanticipated ways. They were going to have to deal with a world in which they had no experience and, as it would turn out, with little help from the federal government that had just given them their freedom.

With the loss of the Confederacy, the southern whites were embittered toward the federal government of the North for the devastation of their land and loss of their way of life. A bitter white aristocracy would look for ways to gain back their way of life and win their lost cause. They would find new ways to economically enslave the freedmen despite the passage of the 13th Amendment.

When the embittered South could not accomplish its mission, it would resort to other means of taking out its anger on the freedmen through many acts of violence. While the two races had formerly lived together in a form of a co-dependent society, now whites would set the former slaves apart from southern society and enact laws to deny the new freedmen their individual rights.

None at the Savannah Oaks plantation that day could foresee all the problems or know how it would end as the slaves were gathered on the front lawn of the main house. They began to move away from the yard, some returning to their cabins not ready to leave. Many, like Josiah, decided to leave the plantation right away.

For Josiah, there was the realization that for the first time in his life, he was free from bondage. But how would he go forth? What would he do now? He had never known anything other than bondage his whole life. Now that he was free, he would have to apply his keen mind to begin to understand what this newfound freedom would mean to him. More importantly, now he would have to find out how he could make a good life for himself in this new different reality.

Without looking back, he walked away from Savannah Oaks and began his search for understanding and a new life.

Illustrations

Fountain in Forsyth Park - Savannah, Georgia

Savannah Oaks plantation mansion - near Natchez, Mississippi

Battle of Antietam - September 17,1862

Andersonville Prison - Ft. Sumter, Georgia

One - Marcus

―――――――◦―――――――

Now, wherever the stars and stripes wave, they protect slavery and represent slavery... This then is the final fruit. In this, all the labors of our statesmen, the blood of our heroes, the lifelong cares and toils of our forefathers, the aspirations of our scholars, the prayers of good men, have finally ended! America the slave breeder and slaveholder!
        - Seth Grahame-Smith

―――――――――――――――――――――――――――――――

Marcus Taylor was born in 1807 in Savannah, Georgia to a wealthy family. His people were of Dutch ancestry tracing back to New Amsterdam in the 1600's. His father Hendrick made his fortune as a cotton factor before Marcus was born. Accountants and brokers were in demand.

He was one of the earliest to prosper from Savannah's role as a major seaport for the cotton business. Shortly after his death, his work, and that of the other early successful factors, would require the completion of the Savannah Cotton Exchange. As the South's king cotton continued to boom, it was built there on Bay Street. Savannah later grew in 1880 to become known as the "Wall Street of the South" before the boll weevil and falling world markets decimated cotton agriculture. Savannah's heyday and decline would come after his day, but Hendrick was one of its pioneers.

Savannah's bustling business hub was perched on a ridge facing north and overlooking River Street and the brisk seagoing activity on the Savannah River. Stone steps were built along the way to descend the steep bluff serving as a levee to the river front.

One

The Taylor family - Hendrick, his wife Jane, Marcus, and his younger sisters Marcy and Constance - lived in a mansion on Columbia Square, originally laid out in 1799. This was one of Savannah's historic squares developed over several decades. They eventually became miniature parks, beautified by live oaks, and with historic monuments and sidewalks running north-south through their centers.

The squares south of Bay Street grew to 24, but began as 4 originally laid out by British General James Oglethorpe in 1733, the same year he founded the colony of Georgia and the city of Savannah. His original plan was to provide space for the colonists to practice military exercises and as vegetable gardens to feed his troops stationed there as a "border" defense in case of invading Spanish from St. Augustine, Florida. James Oglethorpe also established the first Masonic Lodge in America on Bay Street in 1734 at the site that would later become the Savannah Cotton Exchange.

The city was undergoing growth in every direction as expansion tried to keep pace with its commercial successes from king cotton. At the east end of Bay Street, a new road and bridge were under construction to open up Tybee Island to wealthy leisure seekers.

Savannah preserved its history. Fort Pulaski still stood on Tybee with its long history dating back to Oglethorpe and the French and Spanish before his time. Bonaventure Cemetery lay along the Wilmington River to the east of Savannah on the way toward Tybee. Its old graves dated back to the end of the 18th century.

West of the squares, and south below Bay Street, a new city market was opening for outdoor sale of fresh produce and social gathering. At the west end of Bay Street, the bridge over the river to the north led to South Carolina low country, its Sea Islands and Beaufort, the quiet village in the tidewaters.

The beautiful 30 acre Forsyth Park was under construction south of the squares. Neighborhoods south of that were being built for the poorer working folks. These would become the neighborhoods for freedmen after the war. Savannah was a unique city in that it was not as driven by the passions of racism or views of social class as much as most of southern society. As a bustling seaport, Savannah's people were exposed to visitors from European countries and, perhaps more than other southern cities, held a more international perspective. Their very nature was more friendly and inclusive.

More than Savannah, Charleston typified antebellum southern culture and defined the old South. Nearby Savannah, in Georgia, would never reach Charleston's size but would develop its own character. The contrast in societal view between Charleston and Savannah was stark. This was simply understood by the way people greeted strangers. If you visited Charleston, the greeting was "Hi. Where y'all from?" In Savannah it was "Hi. What y'all want to drink?" The Charleston people needed to test your social worthiness by inquiring about your origin and family. The Savannah people weren't concerned with that. They wanted new people to join the party. To say that they were colorful, eccentric, and humorous was to begin to describe them.

People believed that, while Grant struck at Richmond as the capital of the Confederacy, Sherman struck at Atlanta to destroy its heart and soul. But this was not true. Sherman knew that Atlanta was a major strategic target as a railroad hub for Confederate transportation and logistics.

Incorporated as late as 1837, Atlanta didn't participate in antebellum culture. Slave plantations were all over the South, but people would consider them and southern society with an eye on Atlanta. But back then the city was just forming and the region was a frontier with dirt roads and Andrew Jackson's contentions with Cherokee people. The Cherokees were expelled in the sad Trail of Tears. Atlanta would rise from its ashes after the war.

The southern cities on the coast - Charleston and Savannah - had a longer history dating back before the Revolutionary War. They were more developed and the places of southern refinement.

Given the circumstance and nature of the three cities, perhaps Charleston was the seat of southern culture - the notions of chivalry, nobility, aristocracy, gentility, smooth southern charm, courtliness and refined manners - the southern way of life if you were white and wealthy.

Sherman struck Atlanta and burned it to the ground. He followed with Savannah and spared it. He spared Savannah the devastation he had wrought on Atlanta in his march across Georgia to the sea. He left it intact and offered it to President Lincoln as a Christmas present. His troops occupied Savannah and entered unopposed. They seized their cotton, guns and artillery and set up a prison camp on Bay Street. They stayed for several weeks before continuing their scorched earth policy northward to South Carolina.

But long before the war, Savannah was a place of prosperity and gentle indulgence. Marcus grew up with a life that was privileged. His parents provided him the finest education available for his time. But he was not a serious student. He took his unearned position of birth for granted. The work he did with his father gave him a working knowledge of the cotton business - at least from the broker's end of it.

But that did not interest him and he had no passion to follow his father's path for his career, or live under his shadow. He wanted success, to make money, but on his own, his way. He was an ambitious dreamer with delusions of grandeur.

The sailing ships and bustling business activity in Savannah fueled his dreams. But he came to the belief that he would need to seek his fortune elsewhere - somewhere where the competition would favor his own enterprise, where he could exert his own power and autonomy. He witnessed the slave auctions and thought he might strike out to the west and build his own plantation as a cotton producer. That was where the real money was to be made.

Marcus kept his ambitions to himself. He continued to work for his father. For the longest while, this was the easiest way to make a living. And it gave him a freedom to wander about Savannah and think his private thoughts - dream his private dreams.

He enjoyed the city and courting the young women he found. His position in the Savannah society offered him many opportunities to sample the many young women who were looking for a suitable mate to marry, and settle down with, and raise a family. He found them wanting. The truth was that they never found him worthy of marriage. If asked, most would have said that they felt he was a shallow self-centered person, although pleasant enough company.

Hendrick had watched his son grow to manhood. He surely loved him as a man does his only son. But he doubted he had the ability to be successful based on a feeling he had that something was missing. Maybe his ambition was misplaced or unrealistic. He wasn't sure what it was. Somehow he seemed to lack the drive and perseverance.

Hendrick was unaware that Marcus had great ambitions, and so could not know what they were. Marcus continued to work for his father and enjoy the relaxed social life of an eligible bachelor. He continued to dream his dreams.

He met Rebecca Stanley in the riverside park at the east end of Bay Street. He was attracted to this young woman for her elegance and patrician manner. She was tall and thin with beautiful blue eyes and long auburn hair in soft curls. She was the quintessential product of Charleston society and a model example of fine southern womanhood. Her father and brothers had built a manufacturing dynasty in Charleston, supplying the South with work wagons, replacement parts, plows, and hand tools for farming and workshops.

Rebecca was visiting Savannah with her brothers to develop marketing alliances for their products. With her upbringing in the family, she had proven to have a keen head for business and understood how the social graces could win orders and contracts.

She was exercising her foxhound in the park when Marcus approached her. When they began their courtship, Rebecca's older brothers vetted Marcus and found him a worthy companion for their younger sister.

The couple soon formed a comfortable loving relationship and decided to marry. With the blessing of both families, they took their vows in the new First Baptist Church on Chippewa Square. It seemed as though the two rival societies had married and it was a big day for Savannah.

As a boy, Marcus revered his father and wanted to make his own fortune someday when he was able. When he was 28, in 1835, his father staked him in a venture to buy rich land in the west for cotton production. Speculation for new land was competitive by then.

Marcus found his opportunity in Mississippi near the port of Natchez. It was 57 miles east of the port and a one-day trip by horse drawn wagon. It was an ideal location and he bought 650 acres for $7,800.

After he purchased the deed to his plantation, he remembered home and named it Savannah Oaks. Savannah was a major center for slave trade, but practicality demanded he purchase his slaves locally. The Mississippi river was a conduit for the internal slave trade from the upper South to the deep South. He immediately visited Natchez again with the purpose of inquiring about the slaves.

His immediate challenge was labor. Compared to the cost of land, this would be the biggest expense. He talked to local people and learned that slaves could be purchased separately or in lots and conveniently at the same auction with horses, mules and cattle. He found the going price at auction for a prime Negro averaged $1,000.

He learned about an upcoming auction and pondered how to begin. He would eventually require fifty or more slaves for a plantation the size of his. At about $1,000 per head, there was a lot to consider before spending $50,000 all at once for fifty humans.

But to get started, he would have to determine the smaller number needed for the initial work. For right now, the swamp forests would need to be cleared. The timber would be milled for lumber to build the barns, cotton processing buildings and slave cabins to house his human property. He would build a primitive house for himself until the plantation could get started. Sod would need to be broken before the first crop could be seeded. He would need mules and horses. There was a great deal to do.

He returned to Natchez for the scheduled auction he had seen posted on his earlier visit. He had seen slave auctions before in Savannah but *The Forks of the Road* auction here was on a much larger scale with auctions offered more frequently on a continuing basis.

He looked again at the signboard posting the human commodity available for this day's auction. The asking price and the bid price were hardly ever the same. He had to bargain well and spend his father's stake wisely.

Sale of Slaves and Stock

The Negroes and Stock listed below, are a Prime Lot, and belong to the ESTATE OF THE LATE LUTHER McCULLOUGH, and will be sold on Monday, July 20th, 1835, at The Forks of the Road auction, intersection of Liberty Road and Washington Road in Natchez, Mississippi, at 1:00 P.M. The Negroes will be taken to the grounds two days previous to the Sale, so that they may be inspected by prospective buyers.

On account of the low prices listed below, they will be sold for cash only, and must be taken into custody within two hours after sale.

No.	Name	Age	Remarks	Price
1	Sarah	27	Prime Field Hand,	$1,275.00
2	Violet	16	Housework and Nursemaid,	900.00
3	Lizzie	30	Hand, Unsound,	300.00
4	Minda	27	Cotton, Prime Woman,	1,200.00
5	Adam	28	Cotton, Prime Young Man,	1,100.00
6	Abel	41	Cotton Hand, Eyesight Poor,	675.00
7	Tanney	22	Prime Cotton Hand,	950.00
8	Flementina	39	Good Cook, Stiff Knee,	400.00
9	Lanney	34	Prime Cotton Man,	1,000.00
10	Sally	10	Handy in Kitchen,	675.00
11	Ned	46	Prime Man, Good Carpenter,	980.00
12	Dorcas Judy	25	Seamstress, Handy in House,	800.00
13	Happy	60	Blacksmith,	575.00
14	Mowden	15	Prime Cotton Boy,	700.00
15	Bills	21	Handy with Mules,	900.00
16	Theopolis	39	Cotton Hand, Gets Fits,	575.00
17	Coolidge	29	Cotton Hand and Blacksmith	1,275.00
18	Bessie	69	Infirm, Sews,	250.00
19	Infant	1	Strong Likely Boy,	400.00
20	Samson	41	Prime Man, Good with Stock,	975.00
21	Callie May	27	Prime Woman, Cotton,	1,000.00
22	Honey	14	Prime Girl, Hearing Poor,	850.00
23	Angelina	16	Prime Girl, House or Field,	1,000.00

24	Virgil	21	Prime Field Hand,	1,100.00
25	Tom	40	Cotton Hand, Lame Leg,	750.00
26	Noble	11	Handy Boy,	900.00
27	Judge Lesh	55	Prime Blacksmith,	800.00
28	Booster	43	Fair Mason, Unsound,	600.00
29	Big Kate	37	Housekeeper and Nurse,	950.00
30	Melie Ann	19	Housework, Smart Yellow Girl,	1,250.00
31	Coming	19	Prime Cotton Hand,	1,000.00
32	Uncle Tim	60	Fair Hand with Mules,	600.00
33	Abe	27	Prime Cotton Hand,	1,000.00

There will also be offered at this sale, twenty head of Horses and Mules with harness, along with thirty head of Prime Cattle. Slaves will be sold separate, or in lots, as best suits the purchaser. Sale will be held rain or shine.

Marcus had to prioritize and determine what he needed first and most, while pacifying Rebecca's needs. He decided to buy nine Negroes to get started.

Rebecca stayed back in Charleston with her family until Marcus had completed a rough temporary house and begun the major work on the mansion. When this much was ready, he sent for her. When she arrived, she was not happy. The roughness of the land, the oppressiveness of the heat and humidity, and the lack of refinement of the people didn't measure up to Charleston. This place was crude and backward. This was not what she had expected when she married Marcus.

He had promised her, "Rebecca, we will have a great plantation with all the refinements you had known in Charleston." She hoped so.

"When I was growing up, I always wanted a fine home and family of my own and an important place in society."

20

One

There would be a strain in their relationship as time went on.

One

Two - Rebecca

Rebecca Stanley was born in 1809 in Charleston, South Carolina. All the years she was growing up, her family had participated in the high society there. Her father had risen through the degrees of the Free Masons, as had Mozart and Virginians Washington and Madison before him. The social and business connections had enhanced his position and station in society. Her brothers had joined De Molay and would join their father's fraternal Order of Scottish Rites when they were old enough. Her mother belonged to the sister Order of the Eastern Star as she would one day.

The parents belonged to the 1748 St. Andrews Society which met at 70 Meeting Street. They shared this same hall with the 1737 South Carolina Society. There were many other societal organizations in Charleston, including the most prominent St. Cecilia Society. They were all involved in philanthropic causes. The history of their society and its culture was rich and old and deep.

There were gay parties, coming out debutante galas and balls for the upper crust families, seasonal cotillions, celebrated engagements, big wedding affairs, receptions for all the important people on grand lawns with white canopy tents and flowers everywhere. There were mint juleps, merry cheers and toasts, flocks of pretty young ladies twirling in their finest long dresses, older men standing straight and proud, arms crossed, smiling with contentment, watching over them smoking their cigars, and handsome young men excited to begin the courting game.

The splendid architecture, the galleries, the cobblestone streets basked in sea breezes, the wonderful low country food, all brought a fulfillment and great satisfaction to Charleston's people. They loved their lives, filled with gentility and refined courtly manners.

Rebecca had completed her social etiquette training lessons, paid for by her old-moneyed parents. When she was 16, she was presented to Charleston's bachelors and their families at her cotillion. There were escorts, flower girls and pages to attend the grand affair. She had been paired with her beau escort by her parents in agreement with the committee of elite members of society. Her father had formally introduced her to the audience from the stage. She wore a white gown and satin kid gloves and curtsied in the St. James full court manner to receive the invited guests in the line. They had paid for their tickets and this event had charitable benefit for those unfortunate poor souls who weren't invited.

She was eligible to marry. But that was not what she wanted then. She wanted to enjoy her youth and the many beaus who would come to call. The attention and the grand life was the best she could have imagined. Charleston was a joy.

After some years had passed, things changed. She was older. She began to reconsider her life, thought about herself, looked back at and inside of herself, 'Then Charleston was stuffy - saw past this - as after youth began to fade, the courtship game grew tired, boring, too easy, had lost appeal, win was loss, many loves played and forsaken, too many young men's love's lost, while not the right gallant man had come or been found, for too long, it's late, time running out, still none proved strong to make me lose, and put me up high, and cherish as deserved because intelligence was the impediment, no gentlewoman to gentleman man who would do all these things and still make a woman partner, trust and rely on her, let me free to judge, free to decide, rectitude, righteousness and fair, alone love's trials had run its course. I'll inform father, carve out my own path, join the brothers in business, travel, see new places, start new, bide the few years left before spinsterhood is the answer, maybe lower sights, take better aim, settle and lose to win the game in the end.'

That's what she did. Strong-headed she was. Made up her own mind. She traveled through the South with her older brothers to build marketing alliances with distributors of farm and workshop equipment to further develop the family's business. She worked smart and hard, sharing the marketing efforts with her brothers. But the South was a place of ease for the genteel and successful. She often enjoyed its leisure and took respite.

She arrived in Savannah, a short trip from Charleston, and took in the sights of the city. It was different than Charleston. Savannah had grown rapidly at the turn of the century and had more diverse architecture, monuments, statues, refined art, and shops along the riverside quay. There was more of an international flavor to the area with the busy seaport activity on the Savannah River. She had brought her dog and they enjoyed all the beautiful parks and historic squares there together.

She often turned off Bay Street and walked south to St. James Square on the corner of State Street. This was talked about as the most fashionable neighborhood in Savannah. There was a new mansion there she always stopped to admire. The old woman, matron of the estate, was often tending her vegetables on the side yard or flowers in the front. The home was stately, beautiful and imposing.

Two

The morning air was still cool. The flowers sparkled with the dew and soft sunlight rising toward its glorious mid-day brilliance. She took a few moments to compliment the woman on her beautiful Gloriosa daylilies, gardenias, petunias, and Floribunda wild roses. The woman took pride in her garden and appreciated Rebecca's admiration.

Each time, by habit, Rebecca strolled further south to the expansive Forsyth Park beyond the squares. The new fountain there was splendid and a wonder. The whole city was a place of peace and beauty - an urban city yes, but abundant in gentle earthly comforts.

On other occasions, she walked her dog in the park at the east end of Bay Street, looking at the sailing ships moving in and out of the port. She noticed a handsome man watching her from the sidewalk and smiled to herself. She was flattered that she still had the looks to turn heads. And she was amused and gratified - still confident of her charms. She thought, 'Now there's a man I'd like to meet. I mustn't approach him. That wouldn't be proper. I'll bet if I smile at him, he will come over here'. Sure enough, she did and he did.

Marcus approached and smiling back said, "Good day Miss. I saw you and your dog standing here. I wanted to ask if that is a purebred foxhound."

"It is", she replied smiling sweetly with the convincing unbeatable charm that melts the heart of the savage beast.

Struggling for a way to keep the conversation alive, he said, "Do you hunt with him?"

"We have taken him out, but he is mostly a companion in the household."

"Are you from Savannah? I thought I knew all the pretty girls in town."

'Oh, he's a smooth devil', she thought.

"No, I'm visiting here. I'm from Charleston. How about you?"

"I'm born and bred here in Savannah. My name is Marcus Taylor."

"My name is Rebecca Stanley. It's a pleasure Mr. Taylor. Maybe we will see each other again. Good day."

As she moved away, Marcus thought, 'I hope so. I'll see to it.'

Marcus was enchanted with Rebecca, as so many others had been before, and even more, he was smitten. He looked for her in the park everyday. She was never there, but he continued to hope they would meet again.

Then one day, he thought he saw her next to his father's office, near the site the city planners were developing for the future Cotton Exchange. She was descending the stone steps with two older young men down to River Street. The men looked about his age. He couldn't help but wonder and worry whether one or both were her beaus. He was jealous without any justification or earned right.

Two

He thought, 'I must catch her, but cannot appear like I'm following or chasing her.'

He surged ahead with a flimsy plan, and didn't do it well.

He rushed down the stairs and caught up to the Stanleys slightly out of breath and puffed up with his face flushed.

He said, "Rebecca Stanley is that you? I was rushing to meet that incoming ship to discuss the cotton cargo with the captain. But then I saw you and wanted a chance to meet you again."

She didn't believe him but smiled and said, "It's good to see you again Mr. Taylor. These are my brothers, William and Francis. We are traveling together for our father's business. It's good fortune we saw you. We're leaving soon for Charleston. I love your beautiful city. The customers here have been receptive to us and we will be back again."

When Marcus recovered his composure for his awkward advance, he said, "Pleasure to meet you gentlemen. I'm sorry to hear you are leaving. I was meaning to ask you Rebecca, and now you William and Francis as well. Could y'all come to our home for dinner and meet my family?"

Rebecca looked at her brothers and winked.

She smiled at Marcus and said, "Thank you Marcus. May I call you Marcus? We would love to come. It will give us excuse to dally a little longer and enjoy the hospitality of the kind people of Savannah."

He looked too pleased and said, "That's wonderful. Where are you staying? I will send you word."

He said his goodbyes and, as he walked away, thought, 'It will help things go smoother when William and Francis catch a glance at Marcy and Constance.'

Marcus walked toward the dock, pretending to meet the sailing ship.

Rebecca watched him leave, turned toward her brothers, pointed and said with her hand covering a grin, "Looks like that ship is heading full sail out to sea. Marcus won't be able to meet it after all."

They all laughed.

When Rebecca received the embossed linen invitation, she opened it and it read:

Dearest Lady Rebecca and Gentlemen William and Francis:
Our family requests the honor of your presence to
accompany us for dinner on Tuesday eve next at 7
o'clock.
Our coachman will pick you up at 6:45 and bring you here
to Columbia Square.
Without your regrets, we look forward with anticipation
for your acceptance and appearance.
  Warmest Blessings,
  The Taylors

She smiled. Another courtship, maybe the last one, had begun.

The dinner party went well and was a great success. The brothers talked about the family business. Rebecca chimed in. The Taylors were impressed that these young folks, with their tender experience, had such confidence, savvy and ambition. Hendrick wondered if a confident poised young woman like Rebecca would be a good match for Marcus - or even if he would qualify for it. They got to know each other better.

The young men and women enjoyed each other's company and the parents were pleased. The Taylor and Stanley siblings expressed a desire to maintain a cordial friendship. They all noticed Marcus and Rebecca exchange furtive glances when the conversation was at a lull. With warm feelings, the Stanleys left with the coachman and returned to their lodging shortly before midnight.

Rebecca and Marcus met often on Bay Street, in the parks and in the squares. Savannah was a compact city and a pleasure for strollers taking in its beauty. This was Marcus' home and he was proud to squire her around town, showing off Savannah and himself. It didn't bother him a wit - he was flattered for himself as heads turned when they saw them arm in arm.

They often walked south from Bay Street, through the squares, to the gorgeous Forsyth Park with its great fountain. Here they sat and talked long hours about everything - their childhood lives at first, then their hopes, dreams and aspirations. He wanted to impress her with his dreams of being a bigger success than his father. But he was careful with that, didn't want to reveal too much just yet. He feared he might put her off and spoil his chances with her.

Marcus grew fonder of Rebecca and recognized that she was an exceptional woman - intelligent, poised, and an elegant lady with a surprisingly wry sense of humor. But he thought, 'She has high expectations. That will be a challenge for me. She is so lovely and full of life, it will be worth it. No one has ever made me laugh as she has. I can't imagine the rest of my life without her companionship.'

Neither of them was truly young anymore. Time was short and they felt it pressing down like the August humidity in the South. It was time - time to make decisions and move forward. Their courtship was brief.

They sat down on a bench next to the fountain, clasped hands, looked into each other's eyes and sweetly smiled. They had come to a place of mutual love and understanding and decided to marry. He proposed to her on one knee and she was touched by his heartfelt appeal.

She had some doubts but believed it her best choice. She didn't want to lose him. Maybe he would let her lead, maybe not. He didn't seem too bright. With his head in the clouds, he didn't seem too practical. Still maybe this was her best choice - her last choice.

When she didn't answer immediately, Marcus became worried she would say no.

Finally she smiled her Rebecca smile and said, "Yes, I will marry you. I am happy. We must tell our families at once."

He smiled and looked away when it occurred to him, "I know William and Francis, but I have never met your mother and father."

She said, "They will love you, Marcus. We must go to Charleston so that you can meet them. We should stay for a while. They will want to arrange a party to celebrate our engagement."

"Of course, we will go as soon as we visit my folks and tell them our good news. As for the party, I expect they will require it. That's what our folks do."

She laughed and remarked, "It's the only life I have ever known." They both laughed.

They immediately made plans to have dinner with Marcus' family. At the dinner table, so many smiles and furtive looks were exchanged between Rebecca and Marcus that his folks reckoned they had some news to share.

When Marcus told them that Rebecca had agreed to marry him, they were surprised, but acted overjoyed. From the moment they had met her, they had hoped that a romance would blossom between the two young people. Hendrick believed Rebecca's business sense would help Marcus shape his dreams to practical reality. They listened closely, and cautiously, as the couple explained that Rebecca would be sharing the happy news with her family as soon as they could arrange it.

She laughingly told them that she was certain her parents would want to have an engagement party in Charleston right away. The Taylors were delighted to hear this and hopeful Marcus would prove worthy. They were certainly curious about her folks too. They knew the brothers, and the only piece of the puzzle left was the parents. They were sure they would find them delightful. Everyone waited in anticipation.

William and Francis were the first of the Stanleys to hear the news. They were happy for their sister and pleased for the couple. They returned to Charleston soon after the congratulations and told their parents the whole story with enthusiasm. The Taylor elders anxiously awaited the visit from the couple. They were excited for Rebecca and wanted to meet her best beau.

They hoped that Rebecca had finally found the man of her dreams, or so they hoped. There were undercurrents. They had secretly feared that she was bound to end up a spinster. Her independent and strong-willed nature would deny them their grandchildren. The mother had particularly endured the gossip and murmurings about Rebecca's unconventional behavior - taking too long to marry, working as a marketer (little more than a drummer) gallivanting all over the countryside.

When they arrived at the Stanley's estate, William and Francis were the official greeting party. They rushed down the steps to meet them.

Rebecca threw her arms around them and said, "Willy, Fran, I missed my big brothers."

They were happy to see her too.

William smiled at Marcus, kept his eyes on him, while turning his head toward Rebecca and teased, "This man you have brought with you, have you disarmed him?"

"Yes, of course I have. I have completely disarmed him. He is at our mercy."

Marcus finally caught up with the fun and they all laughed. He added for their instruction, and with a grin, "You men will learn this for yourselves one day."

Rebecca's parents were warm and charming and made Marcus feel welcome and comfortable. While they had heard the engagement story from Willy and Fran, they were anxious to hear all the details from Rebecca and Marcus themselves. Before long they were all telling amusing stories and having animated conversations. The young ones recounted their courtship together. The old ones told Marcus delightful and revealing stories of Rebecca's privileged childhood. Marcus thought 'I see where Rebecca had developed her appealing nature from this family.'

After dinner the second evening, the old man spoke to Marcus, "Marcus, let us retire to the study and enjoy some cigars and old Bourbon."

Marcus thought, 'I'd better be mindful' and followed him into the man's sanctuary.

They sat in easy chairs, surrounded by books and fine pieces of art to a man's taste, puffing and sipping, eyeing each other in reflection.

The old man Taylor said, "Marcus, what are your plans for the future after you and Rebecca are married?"

Marcus nervously replied, "Well, I expect we will enjoy some time together in Savannah. I have worked with my father in the cotton business for many years. I could work for him as a factor and take over some day. But I have been thinking about maybe striking out more on my own, something big, maybe in cotton production."

Taylor looked at him askance and said, "I hope you figure it out and get settled before you raise a family. She might be able to help you. Good luck, son."

It was the early spring and Charleston's finest were anxiously awaiting the beginning of their social season. The engagement celebration party fulfilled their expectations. It was splendid, of course. The Stanleys spared no expense. After all, Rebecca was their only daughter and they had waited patiently a very long time for this event.

The house was filled with fresh flowers, the caterers had provided a wonderful buffet and there was a five-piece ensemble playing dance music delightful to their southern heritage. All the cordial finest came to celebrate the planned nuptials of this well raised and bright young couple.

Marcus's folks and sisters came up from Savannah a few days before the important social event so that the two prominent families could became acquainted. With everything they shared in common, they fell into friendship with ease. The Taylors touted Rebecca's virtues and the Stanleys surely approved of young Marcus. They surely hoped he'd be the husband their daughter wanted, deserved and waited for.

Rebecca remained in Charleston for a time to plan her wedding. It was going to be a short engagement. There was a great deal to do in such a brief time. The Stanleys, as the bride's parents, were expecting to hold the grand affair in Charleston. That would be traditional.

Two

But Rebecca was headstrong and favored Savannah. She wanted to make her own decisions - had spent the last few years making her own decisions. This was her affair and the most important day of her life. She was determined that everything about her wedding would be exactly the way she wanted it. She loved Savannah and wanted her wedding there. Her parents graciously conceded and agreed to share the planning with the Taylors.

They married in the late summer of '34. The newspapers in Savannah and Charleston ran articles about the important affair.

The service was held at the First Baptist church on Chippewa Square. The August weather was hot and sticky. It felt close in the church and the people grew impatient. The ladies demurely fanned themselves; the men tugged on their collars. There were tears of joy and lots of perspiration masked with sweet perfume.

Rebecca wore a strikingly beautiful white wedding gown. It was in the Spanish style with lace and a tiara and an ornately beaded bodice followed by a long train. Standing with her father, looking into the church, she prepared to walk down the aisle, and marveled that her wedding was so much like her debutante experiences. She thought, 'This is just like my cotillion. Now I see that was a dress rehearsal for my marriage.'

And poor Marcus, overwhelmed with possibility, stood nervously waiting at the front of the church for his bride. He couldn't believe how lucky he was to have found someone like Rebecca to spend his life with. He gasped with awe at his first view of her walking down the aisle towards him. She was more beautiful than he could ever have imagined.

Two

The reverend instructed them to take their vows and repeat after him, "Do you take this woman ...." "With this ring, I thee wed ...." "I now pronounce you man and wife." The happy couple left the church in a horse drawn carriage, decorated with white flowers and streamers, and headed for the reception.

The layout of the historic district was a unique feature of Savannah. The squares each had a miniature park at its center, surrounded by only four mansions. This made for intimate small neighborhoods. The residents of the mansions would often use the small parks for their own private purposes - neighborhood parties, social gatherings with friends and family affairs, picnics and wedding receptions.

The two families held a large reception - large as they could - in front of the Taylor home. It was hosted together by the Taylors and the Stanleys. The park was decorated with streamers and flowers. Having the wedding in the groom's home town wasn't traditional, but it surely wasn't a problem for Savannah. After all, the thing they loved best was a great party, and this promised to be one of the best. The problem was fitting all the people in the small park in front of the mansion on Columbia Square.

It would be attended by all the important Savannah elites and three neighbors on the square, all the Taylors of course, and all of Rebecca's folks, the Stanleys, and important friends from Charleston. While the cost didn't matter, the family planners struggled to keep the size manageable with the small park in front of their mansion. But with great effort they managed the struggle; the embossed linen invitations were sent out once again, and it was a great affair for both families and Savannah.

Rebecca knew how important her wedding was to her family, so in a spirit of cooperation, appreciation and love for her folks, she agreed to have a second reception back in Charleston. Her father had so many business associates and other socially prominent friends who had known Rebecca all her life and had not been able to come to Savannah due to the restrictions.

After a short honeymoon, the new couple stayed in the big mansion with Marcus's folks and spent the remainder of the summer and most of the fall enjoying Savannah. Marcus continued to work for his father and learn more about the cotton business. There were visits to Charleston and the Stanleys occasionally joined the Taylors for their visits to Savannah. Their lives were happy. They enjoyed their refined southern life with its congeniality and grace.

Rebecca relaxed for a time. This was close to her vision for her adult life - temptingly comfortable, but she missed the excitement of business. There was a lot to consider - partnership as a wife, children, fulfillment in work, and a fine and grand social life.

But the news of the nation's politics was disconcerting. The sectional issues over slavery had fomented troubles in the west. There was growing talk of South Carolina and other states seceding from the Union. There was passionate language and hints of war in the future.

At the end of summer, with the bloom fading on the rose, Marcus told his bride about his ambitions and plans. He told her clearly this time - no hints or equivocations. He had been awkward in the past, and this time was no different.

At a quiet moment he sprang it on her, "I've bought land in Mississippi and will build a plantation."

Her mouth fell open in astonishment, "I thought it was just a dream you had. I didn't think you would do it."

"Early this summer, when you, Willy and Fran were finishing your sales trip back to Charleston, I located good land near Natchez and purchased it. I wanted to make us a fine life with wealth of our own. I promise you I will do that. You will have the grand life with me that you want."

With his father's investment support making it possible, he had pursued his dream on his own, without conferring with her - without her blessing. He entered into their marriage with this deception. He had bought good land far away near the Mississippi River. He would buy slaves and grow cotton.

She was astonished at what he had done and said, "Marcus, how could you? What about Savannah? I thought we were going to establish ourselves here. A cotton factor is one thing, this is another."

He looked at her, saw her concerns and said, "Rebecca, I promise you, it will be all right. When I go to Natchez and begin my work, you will have to stay with your folks in Charleston until I send word for you to come join me. I'm not sure how long it will take, maybe a few months, but I want to have a comfortable place for you first."

She had heard him dream out loud about schemes like this before, while they were courting, but now it was an imminent reality. She grew concerned about the effect this would have on their lives.

Two

Rebecca pouted, looked resigned and said, "I see that is for the best, but I'll miss you dearly."

She knew her life would be ruined.

Three - Josiah

Out of the night that covers me,
Black as the pit from pole to pole,
I thank whatever gods may be
For my unconquerable soul.

In the fell clutch of circumstance
I have not winced nor cried aloud.
Under the bludgeonings of chance
My head is bloody, but unbowed.
Beyond this place of wrath and tears
Looms but the Horror of the shade,
And yet the menace of the years
Finds and shall find me unafraid.

It matters not how strait the gate,
How charged with punishments the scroll,
I am the master of my fate,
I am the captain of my soul

- William Ernest Henley, _Invictus_, 1888

Josiah Ashford was born in 1829 on a plantation in Missouri. By that time most slaves had been born in America from slaves born here also. In most cases it had been generations since they were brought from Africa. The direct link with their heritage and culture had been severed.

His ancestors lived in the west African country of Gambia which was surrounded by the country of Senegal. Well before the 14th century, Muslim merchants had established commercial trade in slavery of its people through trans-

Saharan routes. The Arab culture by the 14th century defined the area as the Mali Empire.

The first Europeans to arrive in the area were the Portuguese in the 15th century. They provided slaves captured in Gambia to Brazil. Dutch, French, German and British came there in the 17th century. Africa sold its people to Europe. Ultimately, the British established the trans-Atlantic slave triangle routes to the Caribbean and the British colonies in North America later in the 17th century. This enterprise lasted for two centuries.

For its indigenous African people, a human was defined by his will to survive. His courage was tested by his bravery to hunt and provide. The symbol of his strength was the heart of the lion. For the human spirit to be human, it must be free. This core belief of humanity would pass on through the centuries.

By the 19th century, America had grown from a country with slaves to become a slave country. By custom, they were given their names from their owners, from biblical or white family sources. Often they had no last names but would gradually be given, or adopt themselves, the family names of the slaveholders.

Josiah's grandfather had been brought from the Caribbean to a plantation in Virginia. He labored there as a tobacco planter under the task system. His son, Josiah's father, had been born there. Years later, Josiah's father was sold to a plantation owner in Missouri. When Josiah was born, the owner had named him Josiah from his recollection of the Old Testament in the Bible. He didn't remember that Josiah had been an ancient Hebrew king of Judah whose name meant "Jehovah saves".

The agriculture on Missouri plantations was a mix of tobacco and hemp crops like the Upper South and short-staple cotton like the Deep South. The slave labor system was also a mix of the more benign task system and the harsher gang system. Josiah's father worked the task system and labored to produce tobacco. But life was not easy for the Negro slaves all the same. They found their solace in worship services on Sundays.

Josiah grew up attending the services which blended the hope for salvation of the Christian belief with the African traditions of the ancestors. The gospel songs they enthusiastically sang were unique Negro spirituals plaintively expressing their angst and sorrow. He sang *Swing low, sweet Chariot* which expressed the longing to be free, and *There is a Balm in Gilead* for the comfort that Jesus heals all who come to him. The congregation stayed after the service for the "ring shouts" which were a carryover tradition from African dance, very expressive, and animated. There was hand clapping, foot tapping and blissful moaning.

He had an insatiable curiosity about life and an African respect and reverence for the wisdom of elders. His father, however, was fully resigned to his station in life and did not look in a forward direction to change his fate as Josiah did. There wasn't much of substance or hope he could learn from the older man. So Josiah watched as time passed and his father grew older and remained resigned to the fate of the enslaved. Salvation did not come in this earthly life. He would have to wait for the next.

His father had long ago given up and, in a contradictory way of reason, inspired Josiah to hope and prepare for the future. When the time came that his father passed, he mourned his father's death but vowed that he would never give up hope or faith in life. His life would be better.

Josiah had strong faith in Divine Providence - that God had a plan He didn't reveal to man. There was a guiding force. The Lord required Josiah to relinquish his will to Him, while God gave him free will for good or ill. As an adult, he came to the view that he was the master of his fate. Free will permitted him to take charge of his life and strive for his own betterment. God's Providence would do what it would do.

The Missouri Compromise of 1820 under President Monroe had sanctioned slavery for the proposed new state. The practice had been established before that. Henry Clay's Compromise of 1850 seemed to offer temporary relief to the growing tensions over slavery in the new territories. But Steven Douglas's Kansas-Nebraska Act of 1854 provoked bloody conflict over the idea of popular sovereignty in those territories.

As the strife over slavery grew in Missouri and surrounding new territories, the plantation owner decided to sell some of his human property and move south. He believed the Deep South would be more secure and protected. He would have to start over. To make that possible, he would have to sell many of his slaves to pay for a smaller parcel of land with the few he kept. The owner bound his slaves with neck collars and shackles and chains on their wrists and ankles and transported them down river from St. Louis to the Mississippi port of Natchez.

Three

Josiah was put up on the auction block there. It was 1852 and he was 23 years old. On the day of the auction, Marcus Taylor bought him as a prime field hand and fair carpenter for $1,150. Many of Marcus's slaves were getting old. In his view, few of the second-generation bred slaves had come into their own to his satisfaction. He regularly visited Natchez looking for an exceptional slave to fulfill his needs.

Marcus made this trip to the auction to look for a Negro that could help Ned, now that his master carpenter was getting older. The plantation was prospering, growing and expanding. He needed more cabins, out-buildings and upgrades. Ned would not be able to keep up single-handedly as the plantation continued to flourish.

He brought his new slave back to Savannah Oaks plantation by horse drawn wagon. The 57 mile trip took all day and they arrived after nightfall.

Marcus pointed over to a cabin and said to Josiah, "You will stay in there with two other field niggers for tonight. Tomorrow morning there will be food for you. The first rule is that you will always speak to me beginning with 'Massa Taylor'. Do you understand nigger?"

Josiah answered quietly, "Yes Massa Taylor."

Marcus smiled cruelly and said, "Good. Don't ever try to run away. Our dogs will catch you and we will bring you back and punish you hard. You will be tied up and lashed until your back is all blood and flayed skin. We will treat your wounds with salt and vinegar if you are still alive after 100 lashes. You will feel more pain than you have ever felt in your life. Do you understand?"

Josiah dropped his head and said, "Yes Massa Taylor. I have the scars on my back from before."

"Let me see your back boy. Make sure you ain't lyin' to me."

He took off his rough cloth shirt and turned around. Marcus looked at the thick scars from his shoulders to the small of his back. "You must have done something bad."

Josiah had been just a young man back at the plantation in Missouri. One of the overseers drove him to town often to help load the wagon with supplies. He overheard two men on the street corner having an animated argument about abolition. With his sense of curiosity, he started walking over toward them. When he drew closer to listen to them, the overseer saw him and became very upset. He didn't want his nigger to take part in these discussions and get thoughts in his head. Just to be certain, he bound Josiah to the pole back at the plantation and gave him twenty lashes.

The lashing was painful, but it didn't change his desire to understand the world outside his isolated existence or his view to improve himself in any manner he could fashion and control. His spirit would never be broken. But he was smart and instinctively understood how to avoid fruitless confrontation and protect himself.

"It was a misunderstanding. I ain't done nothing wrong."

"Let's not have any misunderstandings around here."

Marcus warned him, "Tomorrow overseer Benjamin will set you to work in the field. Obey him always or you will be punished. He is not as kindly as me."

Being a slaveholder for so long had changed him. When he thought about it, he recognized that he was not the same as the young man back in Savannah. His demeanor had taken on a role of arrogant ease and leisure. He took his view of his niggers as matter-of-fact - just as he did his horses.

Marcus had Josiah work the cotton fields for a while until he put his plan in place for him. It helped him establish his authority and achieve submission from his human property. He used the hardship of work in the fields as a device to mold his tool into shape. But he had brought Josiah there with a more important plan in mind. Once he was satisfied with this effort - Josiah gave him no sign that he had failed - he moved him in to live with old Ned. He would now begin his plan to bring more value to the plantation operations.

He said, "Josiah, I want you to apprentice under old Ned and see if you can learn some skills to benefit me."

Josiah responded, "Yes Massa Taylor, I would like to try that. Maybe I can make furniture for you too. That is something I have always wanted to do."

So Josiah began to serve his apprenticeship under old Ned, the plantation carpenter. Ned and Josiah lived and worked together every day. With his father long passed, Josiah soon began to regard Ned as a father. Ned became the elder, dearly respected in the African culture, and someone he could talk to and be free to be himself with. While Ned was completely illiterate, they had many close heartfelt talks about life and faith.

Ned saw intelligence and a thirst in this adopted young son. He became proud of Josiah and hopeful for the young man's future. There might come a day when God would bring his wrath on man and end this sinful shame of bondage.

One of Josiah's duties was to mill timber at the plantation saw mill. He enjoyed this work much and, with Ned's guidance, became expert at making the best cuts to get the most lumber out of each log.

Josiah's practical intellect and interest in self-improvement motivated him to learn everything he could about the nature of wood. He had a pride that searched for affirmation. Ned became his mentor and affirmer. Josiah's thirst for knowledge was quenched by Ned's patient tutelage.

Ned was pleased that Josiah's knowledge of the local wood species - southern pine, pecan, walnut and white oak - had advanced so quickly. With an eye for detail, Josiah studied the grains and figures of wood and aspired to become a fine furniture and cabinetmaker someday. Ned taught him.

One day Josiah was running the saw mill and Ned came out to check on his progress. Josiah saw him approaching and disengaged the conveyor drive and turned off the saw. As the machinery coasted to a stop, it became quiet enough that they could speak to each other.

Josiah said, "How are you today Ned? I'd like you to look at this board on the pile over here and answer somethin' for me."

"I'se doin' fine. What do you wants to know?"

"Well, I look down the edge and lay it down flat liked you showed me."

Ned smiled and asked, "And what's wrong with it?"

Josiah explained, "It's not flat across its width. See the curve?"

"Yep. Sho is not flat. That's called cuppin'. What else you see on them boards?"

"Sometimes they have a big belly along the length like a banana. Sometimes they have a twist along the length."

"That's 'nuther problem. It's called warpin'."

"I think these ain't good enough to make furniture Ned."

"You right 'bout that. But they good 'nuff to make cabins. We can pound 'em flat with nails."

Puzzled by the non-uniformity and inconsistency, Josiah asked again, "Why does wood do this? We mill them all the same."

"When we stack 'em fresh, they are wet. We leave 'em to cure 'til they dry 'nuff."

"But they all don't dry flat, do they?"

"No they don't, we choose 'em for what we need. Some's so bad we hafta scrap 'em for firewood. Some's good for carpentry. The best go into makin' good furniture."

"Thanks Ned. You always help me understand."

Josiah learned. He understood that the artisan could bend wood to his will only so far. As a thinking man, who thought much deeper about things, he knew that this was the same with the master and the slave.

Over the years, he worked with Ned who became like a father to him. They did carpentry repairs to maintain the slave cabins, barns and outbuildings. They built new cabins and did new work upgrading the mansion.

Ned was old and grew sick. When he died, Josiah became the master carpenter of the plantation. Over the years he had learned the many basic skills from Ned.

After Ned's passing, he taught himself the fine points of cabinetmaking and became a skilled furniture maker. This became his passion and fulfillment. He was a valued asset to the plantation.

He wouldn't let his life ebb away as his grandfather and father had done. He knew there was much he did not know, could not even know what there was to know, but was determined to learn and find out what he needed to know.

Despite what others thought and did or controlled, God's Providence, his intelligence, courage, persistence and hard work would prevail in the end. In time, life would get better and he would succeed. Josiah believed that.

Four - Josena

Josena was born in 1837 on the Savannah Oaks plantation. Her mother was Sarah, the feisty field hand that Marcus had bought at his first slave auction in Natchez. He hadn't recognized how much trouble she would be. He only saw her youth and strength. Sarah was one of those slaves that couldn't suppress their resentment. Her nature and spirit would not submit. She couldn't keep her feelings to herself. She always found ways to rebel and show her unwillingness to heal.

Marcus Taylor had begun his work developing his new plantation - an enterprise that was new to his experience. Sarah was a problem. At the beginning, he had left his new bride Rebecca behind in Charleston until Savannah Oaks was sufficiently ready for her to join him. Marcus was busy with all there was to do and lonely without her. As for Sarah, he decided to break her spirit and make her an example.

He stole into her cabin often at night and raped her repeatedly. In this way, he punished her behavior and enhanced his pleasure with his cruel dominance. Josena would be born as the outcome of his authority and his vile, cruel acts.

When she was born, he gave her the Dutch name Josena and favored her. Once she was weaned, he kept her in the plantation main house and raised her as the little mulatto girl of his affection. Everyone on the plantation had known the truth about this. Little needed to be spoken. It wasn't unusual.

Before, when Marcus had completed a rough house as a temporary measure, he had sent for Rebecca. She was immediately disappointed with what she saw. In a short time, she heard gossip and understood what had happened with

Sarah and why she was pregnant. There were few secrets at Savannah Oaks.

When Josena was born, Rebecca knew that this light skinned, yellow girl was the scion of her husband Marcus. She knew where Josena had come from. She seethed with anger, embarrassment, and jealousy and cruelly took out her hatred on little Josena. Confronted with this uncomfortable and disturbing truth every day, she intended to get back at Marcus with a vengeance for his acts of disloyalty. This would become a constant source of pain and their relationship would never be a loving one again as it had been in Savannah. Nevertheless, Josena grew up in the mansion.

———————◦○◦———————

When Marcus brought Josiah to the plantation, he quartered him temporarily with two other field hands in one of the slave cabins. The first morning he was to start to work in the cotton fields, overseer Benjamin brought him out to the yard in front of the main house to gather with the group of slaves. As a new arrival, his wrists and ankles had been shackled the night before. Everyone noticed.

Josena was on the veranda hanging up clothes and saw this new man right away. She noticed how strong and ruggedly handsome he was and the intelligent look about his face. She heard that his name was Josiah.

Once Josiah got over the initial shock and adjustment to his new surroundings - the harsher heat and humidity, the harder work - he noticed the young girl working around the main house as a servant. He heard her name was Josena. Everyone on the plantation called her Josie. He noticed her watching him too and hoped for the chance to see her everyday as he happened by the mansion, or better still, had a carpentry task to do inside.

They took to smiling at each other each time they passed. They got to giving each other a shy little wave. The attraction between them grew. They dreamed about each other - her beautiful face and delicate body, his rugged handsome muscularity. She was coy and flirtatious. He had a sweet smile. She had her mother's spirit that often got her into trouble. He had his resolve to improve his lot in life. The first time they spoke a few words to each, they knew the attraction they felt was real and mutual.

But there was danger in this for both of them. She was Marcus Taylor's daughter. Late one evening Josie carefully and quietly left the house and went to Josiah's cabin. When Josiah opened the door, she stood before him awkwardly and neither of them knew what to say. Their hearts began beating rapidly. This was no dream. This was real.

He backed away and she came inside. They looked at each other a moment longer until she threw her arms around his neck. They kissed passionately. She pressed her body tightly against his and let out a soft moan. They felt his manhood responding. They kissed again, more deeply and urgently. The passion grew quickly for both of them. Their passionate feeling of love turned to lust.

She looked deeply into his eyes, trying to be sure of his trust. Convinced of his goodness, she flashed him a passing glance, looked away and stood back. She slipped her shoulders out of her gown and let it fall to the floor. Josiah gasped and stood back gazing at her naked beauty. He couldn't have imagined how beautiful she looked.

Four

He reached out to her and took her tenderly in his arms. He gently ran his strong hands up and down her arms and strayed to her small perfect breasts. She shivered from the delight of his touch and struggled to breathe.

He picked her up, light as a feather, and placed her gently on his bed. He lay over her looking into her eyes, their eyes locked together. She wrapped her arms around him and caressed his strong back. She winced as she felt the ridges of his deep scars and felt saddened for his suffering. Her instincts were to help him and protect him from pain if she could.

Josiah turned to his side and his hand found her most tender places. Every nerve in her body was on fire and she was overcome with desire. She had never felt this way before. His steady caresses brought her excitement higher and higher. Her breathing grew faster and faster until she gasped and groaned at her completion.

He knew at that moment that he loved her beyond doubt. It was more than he cared for himself. He wanted to continue but wanted to protect her from harm. As the Massa's daughter, she had not seen or felt the cruel reprisal that he had known. She was young and sheltered from the true harshness of slavery.

She looked at him as he grew quiet and gently caressed his strong body. She knew she loved this good man and wanted to be with him always. His honor compelled him to act.

Kissing her tenderly on the lips, he said, "Josie, we have to stop. I don't want to, but we must. You must leave right away. I don't want us to get caught and see you get punished."

She responded, "Don't worry, Marcus won't punish me but I will go because I love you and don't want you to get whipped."

Josie slowly put her gown on as Josiah watched in wonder. After this passionate encounter, they knew that they needed to find a way to get together somehow. And stay together always. They missed each other already.

As Josie walked quickly across the yard, she saw a movement to the side in the shadows. Benjamin had been outside and saw her leave Josiah's cabin. He would report this the first chance he got. He was resentful of the special treatment Marcus gave Josie.

The next morning, Marcus summoned her into his office. He asked her to explain what happened last night. She was never fearful of her father, but feared for Josiah.

She said, "Father, I love Josiah and want to be with him. Please give me your permission to see him."

Marcus couldn't bear the thought of whipping Josie for her transgression. He decided to punish Josiah instead. He knew as master of the plantation that he had to keep control of his slaves and the respect of his overseer.

He instructed Benjamin, "Bind him to the pole in the front yard and give him 25 lashes. Don't punish him with salt and vinegar in his wounds. I need to teach the nigger his lesson but want him to get back to work tomorrow."

After he had thought about it a few days, Marcus saw benefit in permitting the union of Josie and Josiah. She was almost 16 years old and he could not keep her as a little girl anymore. The marriage would provide future offspring and some contentment among the slaves. It might reduce some of the relentless pressure and attitude from his wife Rebecca regarding Josena's irritating presence. The more he thought about it, the more sense it made for the plantation and his marriage.

If he decided they would marry, he would officiate over an informal ceremony. It would not be a church wedding and would have no standing in law as a civil marriage either. He would have them perform the simple African ceremony of holding hands and jumping over a broom placed on the ground. To them, this would symbolize their union. Marcus would always be free to sell them individually in the future should that benefit him.

A few days after he had punished Josiah, Marcus spoke to Josie and Josiah together. He said, "Josie has told me that she loves you and asked me for permission to be with you Josiah. What do you want?"

Looking tenderly at Josie, he said, "Massa Marcus, I love her and want to be with her too."

Marcus asked, "Do you want to get married? That is the only way I can permit you to be together."

They both were overjoyed and said excitedly in unison, "Yes."

Marcus explained his conditions and told them, "After I marry you together, Josie can stay in your cabin at night but must come to the house early each morning to do her work. If she becomes lazy and doesn't do her household chores, I will forbid her from staying with you at night."

That Sunday, Marcus gathered all the slaves and the household together and married Josie and Josiah. The yard was decorated with a trellis of flowers and, for a few moments, everyone on the plantation shared a feeling of happiness for the new bride and groom. Almost everyone.

Rebecca wasn't certain what to think. She had mixed feelings and hoped that this change would take Josie more out of her husband's life. They jumped the broom and everyone applauded.

———————◦———————

After their lovemaking, Josena loved to lie with Josiah at night, snug in their cabin. Their old bed was small but he cradled her in his arms. He stared at the ceiling in the little room, dimly lit from the glow of the oil lamp on the table. His thoughts would wander with imagination and notions about the future.

He asked Josena, "I have a favor to ask you, it is important to me, but dangerous for you."

She turned and looked at his thoughtful face, "If it's somethin' I can do for my lovin' man, I has the courage to do it."

"I know you are brave and love me. I have been thinking. Could you bring me some books from the house without nobody knowing? I have been wanting to do this for a long time."

Four

"I thinks I can. There's some in my father's office. There's more in the empty nursery. Miss Rebecca has some. They's old ones she brought from Savannah. She got new ones sent to her from Charleston. I seen her readin' em."

"If you can do it, without getting caught by her, I'd like to learn to read better. I learned a little bit in Missouri, but we are not supposed to know how to read. Look for a reader not used by them often. Might be able to sneak them out of the empty nursery when she's not around. Be careful. Please bring me one at a time."

She brought him books to read at night, starting with McGuffey's old primary reader, *The Eclectic First Reader*. As his reading improved, he advanced to the popular new books - Hawthorne's *The Scarlet Letter* and *The House of Seven Gables*. Eventually he read Emerson's *Representative Men*, Melville's *Moby Dick* and Stowe's *Uncle Tom's Cabin*.

He learned how to read and learned about the world of ideas. He learned what the world was like outside of plantations and for other people. With a fertile mind like Frederick Douglass, he became self-educated. Unlike Douglass, who expanded his mind as a freedman, Josiah was still a slave.

The year was 1853. Dark clouds were gathering in the southern sky and the storm was coming.

Five - David

It is not the critic who counts; not the man who points out how the strong man stumbles, or where the doer of deeds could have done them better. The credit belongs to the man who is actually in the arena, whose face is marred by dust and sweat and blood; who strives valiantly; who errs, who comes short again and again, because there is no effort without error and shortcoming; but who does actually strive to do the deeds; who knows great enthusiasms, the great devotions; who spends himself in a worthy cause; who at the best knows in the end the triumph of high achievement, and who at the worst, if he fails, at least fails while daring greatly, so that his place shall never be with those cold and timid souls who neither know victory nor defeat.

Theodore Roosevelt from the "The Man in the Arena" section of his speech at the Sorborne in Paris, 1910

David Wexley was born fighting. His people had originated from the same place as Andrew Jackson's and Francis Marion's. They were born and raised in the Carolinas, he in Baltimore, Maryland. But their people came from Ulster in Northern Ireland. They were not Irish. They were the lowland Scottish troublemakers and cattle thieves King James VI sent to Ulster to rid his border of the problems they were causing him. They married with Irish and became the Ulster Scots. In America, they became the Scots-Irish.

They had a long history of hating the English but would pick a fight with anybody if the cause was right. In America, there would come to be differing views of the Scots-Irish. For those who knew, there were two - the racist evil of the KKK founder, Nathan Bedford Forrest II, and the goodness of the tragic hero of freedom at Stirling Bridge, William Wallace. David would embody the second.

He was born in 1832 in Baltimore where his father's folks had settled. Many of the Scots-Irish had settled in the Ridgely's Delight neighborhood during the growing city's first period of expansion in the early 19th century. After they grew to prosperity, the Wexley family had built a grand row house there and moved in next to the many professional people who populated the area. It was a beautiful spot just a short walk to the harbor front, but away from its view.

His father Morgan had been born there also in 1802. Morgan made his money in banking as had his father before him. When David was two years old, his mother suddenly died from an unknown illness. Her heart had simply stopped beating. Morgan never remarried and did his best to raise David without a mother in the household. They were always close and discussed everything together. David revered and respected his father.

They attended Presbyterian church service together all of David's formative years. Morgan believed in helping the less fortunate and contributed generously to the church's missions. Their faith was kind but without a passion for God's direction or presence in their lives.

But for David there was always a void in his life. He lacked for no material comfort, or support from his father, but there was an emptiness. Morgan knew it but couldn't change it. He grieved for their loss himself. There was a prevailing sadness that never went away.

As a young boy, David was a good student, attentive and eager to learn. He received a good grounding in the classics and shared his father's passion for history. Morgan discussed with him the significance of the long history of the European old world and its impact on the brief history of the new world here in America. They enjoyed their Socratic debates about the value of history for its ideas and meanings for mankind.

Morgan told him about witnessing the British naval attack on Baltimore harbor when he had been a young boy. The citizens of Baltimore watched the bombardment of the British ships and Ft. McHenry, back and forth, into the night. The British were defeated and the harbor was successfully defended. The flag still flew over the fort in the morning. It was named after James McHenry, a Scots-Irish immigrant and surgeon-soldier.

David grew up a restless boy who always longed for adventure. In his youth, he read all the great epic works - fiction and non fiction - of action, adventure, exotic foreign places, the great military men and war. He was imaginative and lonely. He thought about becoming a writer, or a traveler or a soldier. He talked to his father about history and politics and would later become a journal writer. He was one of some young men who would leave the quiet life of the privileged father for life on his own terms. He wanted to strike out on his own and see the world. Morgan understood that David would not follow him in the banking business.

When David was 16, and with Morgan's blessing, he joined the Merchant Marines and sailed topsail schooners - Baltimore clippers - out of Baltimore and along the Atlantic coast to ports in Boston, Charleston, and Savannah. He learned about the societal views and culture of southern people in Charleston and Savannah, and how they differed from Baltimore and even from each other.

At sea, British impressment of American sailors had continued long after the War of 1812 and he saw some naval battle action himself. With an abundance of time at sea, David began keeping a journal of his experiences and thoughts - sometimes expressed very personally and poetically. Life at sea could be very lonely; it brought back memories of his childhood.

He wrote of sadness and how it had become a warm companion. It was something he had become accustomed to. At ports-of-call, he often posted letters to his father to continue his lifelong habit of sharing his views with him. But his journal entries were mostly his private thoughts he kept to himself.

Journal entry, July 12, 1849-

Made port-of-call to Boston Harbour. Much more than Baltimore, this old city housed the first American rebels – the Adams's, Revere, Hancock and Paine – patriots all. Massachusetts was surely the colony of troublemakers for old King George. The place still reverberates with the ghosts of these great freedom fighters.

I feel a strong kinship with these great men. Somehow injustice, whether it was in the past or in the present, seems to stir feelings of rage within me. I can't explain the strong hatred of injustice I feel, where it comes from, or how I can abide with it. Sometimes I imagine myself to be

like my ancestors – the clans in the Highlands
in their tartan kilts with their sgian-dubh short
knives in their hose fighting the English with
their broadswords and pikes.

The people are serious minded merchants with
some of the Puritan blood still flowing in their
veins. They are honest, decent and forthright. I'd
be proud to be like them.

Journal entry, September 4, 1850-

At sea, we have to keep a close lookout for
trouble. We are charged to protect and secure the
safety of our cargo and the important passengers
we often carry. We met a British privateer off
Cape Hatteras.

Our lad in the crows nest on the focsle saw
them with his spyglass and reported they were
flying British colors. When she closed to 100
yards, she struck the skeleton and crossbones
and we knew she was up to no good.

As the privateer closed in, she fired a warning
shot over our bow. We answered with a flurry of
our cannon shot through their sails. They took
our intent and sped off. After the powder smoke
cleared off our cannon, the boys on the main-
deck cheered our victory for this very short
battle.

Five

Journal entry, August 4, 1851-

We sailed into the port of Charleston for a two day layover. The town has beautiful neighborhood areas, away from the wharfs, where the old Revolutionary War homes are preserved. There is a lot of southern colonial history in this place.

The South Carolina people hold a very independent view and I expect they will cause trouble for America before long. They have their own elite view of high society I find noxious to my taste. Their refined airs remind me of strutting peacocks showing off their colorful tail feathers.

Journal entry, October 16, 1851-

Made port at Savannah, Georgia. To my surprise, the people here are more down to earth than their neighbors in Charleston. Like Charleston, there is Revolutionary War history here as well. There is an old fort out toward Tybee Island and unique squares below the main street next to the river front.

They love their southern culture, but have more of a humor about it. They don't take themselves so seriously or think themselves so self important.

I delighted in visiting their fair city and enjoyed some mirth and drinks on their river front. I felt at home in the taverns. Sailors are sailors and people are people everywhere that you go in the world.

I also witnessed a slave auction near the city market and could not believe that human beings could sell other human beings as a commodity in such an unfeeling and nonchalant manner. The prices were posted on the building for the buyers to shop for their humans and farm animals. The South is a different world.

Journal entry, March 12, 1852, after visiting Charleston and Savannah -

The southern way of life includes an affectionate flavor of courtly manners. I find it endearing and a comforting delight, and can find nothing wrong with it. The manners are related to the language. It goes way back, like we were in the North during colonial times. It's old and elegant the way we talked and behaved.

On the return leg to Baltimore of his final voyage, October 14, 1853 he wrote-

The vast ocean is a cold and selfish mistress. She deceives with her lies that she makes me free. She roils and crashes in angry rage or lays in quiet passive calm. Her two moods are only for herself. She gives no comfort to me. I have only myself as my warm companion for this life's loneliness.

The open sea had once appealed to his nature, but after a few years he resigned his commission and came back to Baltimore, ready to move on to something else. He stayed with his father in the row house in Ridgely's Delight, but valued his independent spirit too much to work for wages in a factory. He had learned as a shipmate that he enjoyed creating and building things with his own hands.

David took an apprenticeship as a carpenter and soon practiced his new skills working with a crew that build houses in the growing city. Their crew built the frames and did the roofing for new construction of residences and businesses throughout Baltimore's urban neighborhoods. Other crews followed after them and did the lighter finish work.

The boss of the crew, who trained him, was a man named Geoff Braxton. He was a master carpenter and from Baltimore also. He was a big beefy man of medium stature, but hard muscled from many years of heavy-frame carpentry. His appearance was a contrast to David's taller, more wiry frame.

They hadn't met before and Geoff was five years older than David. As was customary with many tradesmen, they started the job early in the morning, just after sunrise, to accomplish as much as possible while it was still cool. They picked up their tools and knocked off work mid-afternoon when the heat grew most oppressive.

Most days the crew spent the late afternoons in the local taverns and enjoyed each others company over several pints of beer and tavern food. This had been a customary way for working-class men to socialize that dated back to the earliest American colonial days and before that in the English pubs. Men from all the trades - the carpenters, the masons, the shipbuilders, the coopers, the riggers - gathered together and shared the male companionship at the taverns. It reminded him of his brief visit to Savannah.

Geoff was affable, always smiling, and liked to talk. He led the conversations and soon learned that David was intelligent and more worldly-wise than his younger years would have suggested. They became friends and respected each others' views. They talked about everything - women, politics, religion, and of course building construction. Usually the talk came around to the state of affairs in America. The subject was on everyone's minds. In Maryland, like the other border states on the Mason-Dixon Line, not everyone agreed where the country was headed or what should be done about its problems.

On occasion, Geoff came over to David's home for dinner with him and his father. He quickly learned from the dinner conversation with the old man where David's intelligence and knowledge of the country's politics had come from. He listened in amazement as they exchanged the latest news circulating in the newspapers and on the street. He recognized they were more aware and informed than many on the street.

One afternoon, when they were picking up their tools for the day, Geoff told David, "There's trouble in the country. The southerners are goin' to pick a fight before long."

David agreed, "I know it too Geoff. You've heard me and my father discussing it. I read the newspaper articles and it don't look good."

"If it comes to it, we will lick 'em easy and put down any rebellion they try in short order", Geoff concluded.

"I hope you're right. We can't know how deep the resolve of the southerners will go. The folks I met in the South won't give up their way of life easily. I think the aristocrats, and I suppose the poor folks, will fight for their rights to the death."

David enjoyed the work, his friendships with the crew, and the freedom to move around the neighborhoods of Baltimore and work outdoors with them. But for him, this was still a confinement. The city wouldn't hold him for long. He had seen other people in other places and couldn't stand still forever.

He had a problem with authority. It didn't come from Morgan. His father had always given him free reign to become what he would become. David's worldview would serve him well throughout his life, but in the end, it never brought him happiness.

———————————————————

Morgan Wexley was sitting in the old leather chair behind his big mahogany desk in his front room study. He was working on some papers and had been watching out his window at the sparkling morning sun in his beautiful neighborhood. The flag over Ft. McHenry was visible on the harbor in the far distance.

Morgan had become concerned, and then despondent, about the country's politics. David came into the office to greet him a good morning.

Morgan looked up and responded, "There is going to be war, David. It's unavoidable. The moderates of the North and South have been silenced by the roar of the firebrands."

"I know father. I have been following *The Liberator* and Garrison will keep pushing for abolition without compromise. Emancipation with no plan for the aftermath."

"Worse than that David is John Brown. That wild-eyed madman caused bloody violence in Kansas and a foolhardy attack on Harper's Ferry Arsenal. He is plum crazy."

"The southerners are no better father. They are committed to their system of slavery and their idea of honor. The short-sighted fools keep making money on cotton and won't invest in manufacturing.

I read the old newspaper articles in The Cincinnati Gazette and the New York Evening Post from '56 about the Brooks-Sumner affair. Senator Charles Sumner was sitting at his desk in the Senate Chambers when Congressman Preston Brooks beat him over the head with his thick gutta-percha cane and knocked him to the floor, blinded with his blood on his face. He continued to beat him, wanting to kill him, until his cane broke. This was all about Sumner's abolitionist speech, 'Bleeding-Kansas', his denouncement of the Kansas-Nebraska Act and personal insults toward Brooks' family. When senators rushed to help him, Laurence Keitt blocked them, pointed his pistol at them, and demanded they let them be. After that, the southern senators passed out canes to commemorate their glorious act in defense of southern honor and wore side-arms to insure peaceful conduct of their astute deliberations."

Morgan continued, "They have tried everything to keep their way of life going. Senator Calhoun's gambit for South Carolina's nullification of tariff disadvantages, the positive good of their peculiar institution, Douglas's ploy for popular sovereignty in the west. Even moderates like Senator

Crittenden made a last ditch effort to compromise and bend over backwards to appease the southerners one last time. None of it worked. Colonel Robert E. Lee had hoped Christianity would resolve the slave issue, but it hasn't.

Look at this old newspaper clipping I saved back when President Buchanan took office in '57. The abolitionists were livid about the Dred Scott Supreme Court decision. This is an editorial from the *New York Tribune*. You know I agree with them in their spirit, but think about the trouble it caused."

David read it and replied, "So do I most for certain. But that's very discouraging. It appears hopeless. President Lincoln wants to preserve the Union above all else. He wants to end slavery too, and has offered ideas to compensate the southerners for their economic loss. Nobody is listening to him. The radical southerners and northerners hate him and don't care."

Morgan looked crestfallen and said, "David, listen to the words of Harriet Beecher Stowe." He read them to him:

A day of grace is held out to us. Both North and South have been guilty before God; and the Christian church has a heavy account to answer. Not by combining together to protect injustice and cruelty, and making a common capital of sin, is this Union to be saved, but by repentance, justice and mercy; for, not surer is the eternal law by which the millstone sinks in the ocean, than the stronger law, by which injustice and cruelty shall bring on nations the wrath of Almighty God!

"Throughout history man has always practiced slavery, the powerful subjugating the weak. But in America we have

70

institutionalized it, become dependent upon it to fulfill our agrarian vision for our society and economy. It has become a greater thing than man has ever known before. Now we are justifying it. I don't know whether we will suffer God's wrath or reap what we have sown without Him, but the time to pay for it has come. The price will be horrific.

It's too late David. Hatred is imbued in both our societies. After decades of sectionalism and political wrangling and partisanship and compromises to delay it, now it comes to war."

The people in Baltimore heard about South Carolina seceding from the Union, followed by six other states, after Lincoln's election. The Civil War had begun with P.G.T. Beauregard's bombardment on Ft. Sumter, defended under the command of Major Anderson, in Charleston harbor in 1861.

David was 29 years old. He held the view that the southern aristocratic planters and slaveholders were descendents of the royal English noblemen his people despised. They were the nobles with their fiefdoms, fed by the enslaved peasants. The specter of hating and rebelling against upper-class nobility and cruel authority raised its pugnacious Scots-Irish head again. He would be in for the fight of his life.

Maryland was a border state and divided on slavery. Here, like in the other border states, brothers often signed up to fight against brothers. The choice was not a simple matter of good versus evil. David joined with those who would fight for the Union Army of the Potomac. Geoff and David signed up with Baltimore's Light Guard Infantry. Their outfit joined with others and would fight under the command of Ambrose Burnside from Rhode Island.

They met Patrick Allister with the Massachusetts 17th Regiment Infantry. Patrick was a serious-minded patriot coming from that long tradition in New England. They were issued their new 1861 Springfield, percussion cap, rifle-muskets and trained together in Baltimore for three months and learned how to drill, follow orders and use their weapons. Many men were in poor shape and needed to develop physical conditioning, but for the three of them, that was not a challenge. Patrick was an experienced hunter and taught David and Geoff what he had learned growing up with firearms and hunting and tracking large game in the woods.

The three of them spent their spare time together drinking and laughing in the taverns, awaiting their deployment. Patrick and David's friendship grew from their shared common knowledge of seafarers - Patrick's New England heritage and David's experience as a merchant sailor. Together they often entertained the men, arm in arm and under the weather, singing a duet of their favorite sea chantey - *The Sailor Likes the Bottle - O*. The men spent many happy nights - drinking and singing - in male bonding and companionship.

Always together, they were hail fellows well met at the end of their callow youth, celebrating gaily and excitedly before a war starts, unaware of the horror they were about to face before the killing and sadness begins, not knowing the difference between victory and despair, or when youth, with its innocence, is gone and forgiveness is sought for the remainder of their lives.

But the time came soon when they went off to war. It looked like their regiments would go to Virginia to whip the Rebels on their home ground. It was an exciting time for adventuresome young men. They left with Burnside's Expeditionary Corps in the late summer of '62. They would follow the campaigns of George McClellan and George Meade.

When he left Baltimore, David's father had bade him farewell, "Take care my son. I pray that you get through it and come back in one piece. Fair thee well."

"Thank you father. I love you. Be well."

For all he had learned and understood, not enough of love, he could not know the true source of his nature or where it would lead him. At its deepest root, from the long distant centuries past, and an ocean away, it was the spirit of Wallace - the warrior poet. It was the brilliant and beautiful sadness, so rarely understood. It was a view of injustice and the courage and conviction to fight against cruel authority. Awareness is not knowing. David was aware but would never know that was who he was.

Five

Six - The Battles in the East

For its final campaigns, and more clearly defined than the earlier years in the east and the west, there were two major forces of will guiding the actions of the Civil War.

Lee was guided by his personal belief in God's will. He felt God's presence always and accepted his losses and victories in this way. Most days he sought solace from God for the tragic loss of his best friend and ally, Tom Jackson. This gave him his confidence and his peace, borne by humility, to persist. Lee had hoped that the South would remain united. But the men in the Carolinas and Georgia drifted away from the fight and went home. All Lee had left were the loyal men of Virginia.

Grant was guided by the will of Abraham Lincoln. Ultimately, Lincoln chose him and gave him a free hand to run the war. He was pragmatic and believed in the superiority of the numbers and the equipment. He staked his fortunes on attrition. He knew the Union had the strength. The Union would prevail some day.

For both Lee and Grant there was a dignity and a character that defined what a man would do. It was the total of their honor, their pride, their integrity, their word. If they said it to their men, they could not let themselves fail. This was true leadership. It would survive their deaths and be the way they could both triumph.

But for Lee and Grant, and everyone, there was a weariness that prevailed over the mood of the country. David Wexley fought in several campaigns - in Maryland and Virginia - for the Union Army of the Potomac and soon fell into that feeling.

---○---

Antietam - September 17, 1862

Ambrose Burnside was a large, physically imposing figure of a man. His distinctive style of facial hair became known as sideburns as a derivation of his last name. He was born in Liberty, Indiana of Scottish ancestry. His father had been a native of South Carolina and a slave owner.

His interest in military affairs and his father's influence led to his appointment to West Point where he graduated 18th in the class of 1847 as a brevet second lieutenant. He participated in the end of the Mexican-American war and western campaigns. Eventually he served in Rhode Island where he met his wife.

He resigned his commission for a time and participated in firearm manufacturing, the railroad industry and politics. He became a friend of George McClellan, and later served under him when he rejoined the army at the outbreak of the Civil War.

He was a brigadier general in the Rhode Island militia. After commanding a brigade without distinction in the First Battle of Bull Run, he became a brigade trainer for the new Army of the Potomac. In the battle of Antietam, he was assigned command of the right flank of the Army of the Potomac under command of McClellan.

While he was personally popular and well liked, his military reputation was less positive. Inexplicably, and even ironically given his own proclivity for delay, McClellan was upset that Burnside was hesitant to act when ordered to attack. His delaying tactic allowed time for A.P. Hill to arrive from Harpers

Ferry and repulse the Union breakthrough. McClellan refused to supply Burnside with reinforcements and the battle ended in a tactical stalemate.

Grant found him unfit for the command of an army. Burnside understood himself that this was true. He had twice refused command of the Army of the Potomac and only accepted when told the alternative would be Joseph Hooker.

— ∘ —

Early in the war, General George McClellan led the Union army as general-in-chief and organized the Army of the Potomac. In time, President Lincoln came to view him as too tentative and hesitant to seize advantage when opportunity for victory was presented. Eventually Lincoln replaced him.

Lee had taken full advantage of McClellan's hesitancy and it accounted for his early victories in Virginia. But with McClellan replaced, Lee lost the advantage and suffered poorly in the later battles.

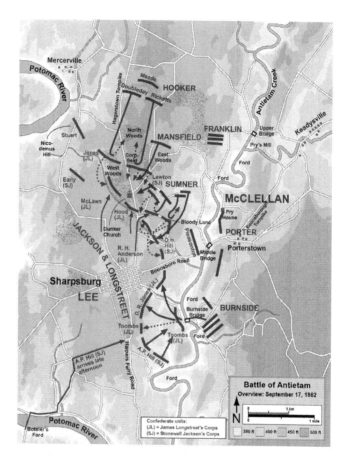

Battle of Antietam
Overview: September 17, 1862

Confederate units:
(JL) = James Longstreet's Corps
(SJ) = Stonewall Jackson's Corps

Union General Burnside played a key role in the battle of Antietam under the overall command of General McClellan. David had fought with Burnside's men.

Near Sharpsburg, Maryland, fighting had begun in a cornfield bordered by two stands of trees. At first Confederate General A.P. Hill used a sunken road as a defensive position and the Union was driven back. Then, because of confused orders, the Confederates lost advantage and fell back. Burnside followed orders to capture the arched stone bridge that spanned Antietam Creek. It would later be called the Burnside Bridge. It looked like the Union was going to prevail as they moved against both flanks of the Confederates and their center was broken at the sunken road.

As the Yankees pushed across Antietam Creek, they turned the Confederates' flank. Hill's forces arrived to stave off total defeat. Over several hours, he drove the Union back. David didn't see him, but Geoff Braxton was with the crowded blue wave crossing the Burnside Bridge. Halted and standing at the center of the bridge, Geoff saw the muzzle flash singled out from the enemy, felt the thud of the ball strike his chest, uttered an inaudible soft grunt, thought, didn't have time to feel, the excruciating pain in the core of his body, collapsed to the ground and his life was gone in that instant.

David eluded capture and fell back with the men as they retreated over the bridge. General Rodman was killed and the Union forces became demoralized. Stuart arrived, with Lee accompanying him on the Harpers Ferry road, to assist the Confederates.

———————————∋●⊂———————————

General J.E.B. Stuart was most often called Jeb Stuart from the initials of his given names. He was Lee's secret weapon. Lee relied on his leadership of the cavalry to gather information from the front and lead gallant surprise skirmishes to disrupt the enemy. He moved his cavalry rapidly and appeared suddenly to the enemy's dismay.

Some called him Beauty from his time with his classmates at the United States Military Academy at West Point. His class rank was in the highest and he could have served in the elite Corps of Engineers. But he went with those of the second rank, to the cavalry, and excelled to the pinnacle of that throng. He was a born horseman in southern Virginia and of Scots-Irish descent.

Most everyone who stood out at the Point was given a nickname there, one that suited them in the view of their friends. William Tecumseh Sherman was nicknamed Cump because of his unusual middle name. Philip Sheridan was called Little Phil because of his small stature.

Northern and southern cadets were there together before the war. They had graduated as brevet second lieutenants and many had fought together as junior officers in the Mexican War, the frontier conflicts with Native Americans and the antebellum violence in Bleeding Kansas. They had enjoyed each other's camaraderie at the Point and would reminisce about those days of their youth, and the spirit of duty and the corps, for the rest of their lives.

Beauty was very plain looking but with a confident, flamboyant personality. His infectious spirit charmed his fellow officers and his men. The men would cheer, smile and say, "There goes Beauty" when he rode by - bold, gallant, chivalrous, tall and erect in the saddle, brandishing his saber in the air, his felt hat folded up on one side, his colorful bushy flowing ostrich plume flying above it, his bright yellow sash, often a red flower in his lapel, his red lined cape floating behind him.

The southern women loved him - his courtly bows, his chivalrous flourishes. He was an inspiration to the Confederates and Lee was deeply saddened when he was killed. He missed him almost as much as his closest friend, Tom

Six

Jackson. Lee loved them and sought God's solace for his loss of them both.

———————◦———————

The Union regrouped on the other side of the creek. With less than an hour of daylight remaining, the engagement of the men and the artillery ceased until the morning. On the night of the 18th, the Confederates withdrew across the Potomac at Botelier's Ford back into Virginia.

The battle was considered a draw. Lee was not victorious. McClellan let him slip away and retreat back into Virginia. The Army of Northern Virginia gave up its ambitions to bring the war to northern territory for now. There would be one more attempt in Pennsylvania at Gettysburg.

Here, on this day at Antietam, 24,000 were dead, mortally wounded, captured or missing. The Union killed and wounded were nearly 12,000. The Confederate killed and wounded were over 9,000. The madness of Antietam was that the men didn't have a fighting chance. Too many died. Their officer's view was that they died with honor and were heroic. It was, in reality, tragic.

On September 22, 1862, after visiting the Antietam battlefield, President Lincoln issued a preliminary Emancipation Proclamation. Now the war was officially about abolishing slavery as well as preserving the Union.

Corporal David Wexley got through it without a scratch. He had lost sight of Geoff but learned later that he had fallen during the charge over the Burnside Bridge, had been shot in the chest and died instantly.

Six

He wrote his father every chance that he could and reassured him that, "The fight is tougher than we could ever have imagined. Take heart and be reassured, I am alive and well. I can't have any certainty when it will be over."

He decided not to tell his father about Geoff.

He wrote in his journal on September 19th-

Father's vision was prophetic. Man has brought his own wrath upon himself. The price was horrific. We have not yet seen how much greater the price will be or how much more slaughter there will be to come. When it ends, I pray it will have been worth it.

Battle of the Wilderness - May 5-7, 1864
This would be David's final fight - Grant's overland campaign to capture Richmond, the capital of the Confederacy. After his successful campaign in the west, Lincoln met Grant in Washington to discuss the remainder of the war in Virginia. Lincoln chose Grant to lead the Union forces.

Grant made peace with his rival, George Meade and left him his command of the east. Meade had graduated from West Point in 1835; Grant in 1843. Both were brilliant military strategists.

Meade disagreed with Grant's philosophy of accepting heavy casualties to win the war by attrition. But, since Lincoln had chosen him, Meade did the honorable thing and offered his resignation. Grant refused to accept it and they agreed to form an alliance with Meade subservient.

They may have been rivals with battling egos, but they made accommodation for each other and honored each other's dedication to duty. Both agreed the true objective was Lee, not Richmond. However, at the Wilderness, Lee's Confederate Army of Northern Virginia successfully outmaneuvered and repulsed them and won a tactical victory.

Both armies' command structures were broken down in traditional hierarchy - corps, divisions, brigades. A majority of the commanders on both sides had been together and shared their military knowledge from West Point.

Union forces under Grant included Generals Hancock, Sigel, Meade, Butler, Warren, Sedgwick, and Burnside. McClellan had been de-commissioned by Lincoln earlier in the war. Confederate Generals under Lee included Ewell, Stuart, Anderson, A.P. Hill and eventually Longstreet. Jackson had been lost to friendly fire a year before.

Meade had previously attacked Lee's army north of Richmond. On the second day of the fight in the Wilderness, Burnside moved south from the Turnpike toward the Plank Road to confront A.P. Hill. Hancock joined Burnside and assaulted Hill there. Hill's troops became exhausted. Lee waited impatiently for Longstreet to arrive and relieve him. Longstreet arrived when it was over.

David fought under Burnside again. They attacked the Wilderness from the north along Germanna Ford on May 4th. At the time, the Orange Turnpike and the Plank Road joined and pointed east toward Fredericksburg, Virginia in the forested area known as the Wilderness. The unfinished railroad ran east-west and south of there.

Picket lines were positioned on both sides of the Turnpike and spread out on the edge of a wide field.

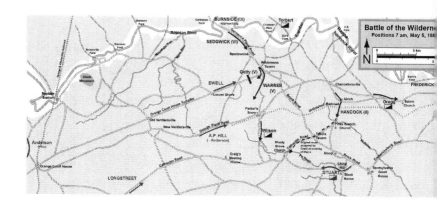

Movement inside the tangled forest was confused as the infantry on both sides had no clear view. Artillery and cavalry were ineffective. The commanders had poor field intelligence and could not form up and lead their forces effectively. Given the number of them, coordination was complex. Lee and Grant persisted.

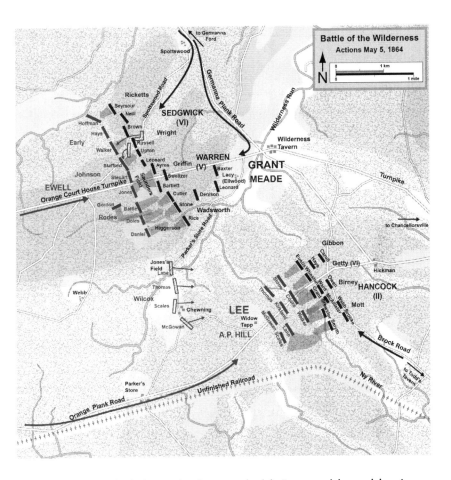

David struggled through the tangled briars and brambles in the woods. He was finding, like everyone in his company, that these were much more than a nuisance. His progress was not only slowed down, but he was cut up and bleeding from deep scratch wounds as he pushed closer to the Confederates. Just the effort to move ahead was exhausting.

The exchange of musket fire and occasional artillery was so intense at one point that it ignited the woods on fire. The men became terrified that they would be burned to death before they could meet the more honorable death from the enemy's bullet.

It was afternoon, but David could barely see his way through the haze from the wood smoke and clouds of black powder. The daylight looked to him like a thick morning haze. His comrades were invisible and if he hadn't heard their voices shouting, he would have felt he was fighting alone.

He chased surreal moving figures, with only parts of bodies visible like dismembered ghosts. He tripped and stumbled often on the uneven terrain. There were dropped logs and limbs in his path. He stepped on lumps that were the silent fresh corpses of the fallen from both sides. The unseen wounded shouted out in pain, desperate for help.

Suddenly the haze cleared and David saw three Rebels charging at him through the trees, closing the distance between them too rapidly. He was unable to reload his Springfield rifle-musket in time to fire at them. With bayonet fixed, he would have to take them on in hand-to-hand close fighting.

He swung his rifle as a club and knocked down the first to reach him. Just in time, he wheeled around and ran the second Rebel through the chest with his bayonet. He ducked just as the third one swung his musket butt at his head, tripped and fell on the ground. The Rebel stood over him, poised to drive his bayonet into David's chest. A Union comrade appeared from behind the trees and fired his musket at the remaining Rebel. The minie' ball blew the back of his head off and he was dead before his body landed on the ground.

Six

David got up and ran out of the woods with the reformed blue wave. With fear and panic on their faces, they met the enemy on the open field. There, unlike the concealment and chaos in the woods, men were mowed down with brutal and greater efficiency. Now the artillery could participate to increase the carnage. The Union killed and wounded were over 14,000. Confederate total casualties were about 8,000.

David was in the thick of it and caught a minie' ball in the left leg from a rebel sniper 150 yards from his position. The bullet entered his thigh, grazed and cracked his femur bone and ripped through his hamstring muscle with profuse bleeding at the exit wound.

He screamed with excruciating pain as he fell to the ground, was unable to retreat, and became part of the carnage. He was one of 12,000 Union wounded and over 3,000 captured or missing. For David, it was done. He would not see the perfect slaughter of Cold Harbor and the others to follow.

As darkness fell, he lay on the field with the thousands of the dead and wounded. It was quiet after the cannon and muskets had ceased firing. The ghosts kept company with the wounded and suffering. It was so still. There was only the sound of the moans and cries for help from the living and those still to die.

The bullet had missed his femoral artery or he would have bled out in minutes. He went into shock and fainted. The Confederate medical and burial squads sorted through the blood and the bodies. They found David unconscious but alive and breathing.

Six

For those charged with the aftermath, the scene was chaotic and the triage was overwhelming.

One of the squad shouted, "Over here. There's one alive. This one's a Yankee."

A medic came over and said, "Hold the lantern so I can see. His pant leg is soaked with blood."

He took the scissors out of his medical bag and cut off the soaked cloth.

"Put a tourniquet above the wound up here. Twist it tight. Bring over a stretcher."

They carried him to one of the horse-drawn ambulances and took him, along with many, to one of the hospitals in Richmond southeast of there. Many died on the 65-mile journey before they could get there.

During the aftermath of the devastating battles of the Civil War, a spiritual concentration occurred, of a magnitude rarely before at one time and one place since man's time on earth, as hosts of angels descended to American soil. As Enoch had described, the truth of the heavens was revealed as they intervened.

The four highest leaders of the seven Archangels - the second phylum with Michael from the south of fire, Raphael from the east of air, Uriel from the north of earth, and Gabriel from the west of water - worked together this once as allying generals and mustered and directed a great third army to descend to the earthy battlefields.

Six

Hundreds of pale clouds of white light filled the black night. A dense feeling of electricity filled the cool night air and changed it profoundly. Sounds of the Cherubim and Seraphim - the third and fourth level of angels and most joyous phylum - fell upon the human spirits departing and joined their voices together to sing beautiful music for comfort and reassurance and assistance to the many dying and just-dead human beings, at the moment of the end of their earthly lives, for their last march - their last journey.

The Powers - fifth phylum - joined the others and with their energy, brought healing from the electrical force of their beings and healed the bodies on the ground cell by cell.

The Carrions - sixth phylum - escorted away the dark entities. The Virtues - seventh phylum - made the necessary changes, unknown to the living, to the charts of records of their lives. The ninth and tenth last phylums - the Thrones and Principalities - came as the Mother and Father Gods to warn and protect and guard against danger.

A funnel, like an inverted tornado, held fast to the ground, pierced a bright hole in the sky and lifted thousands of the fallen blue and the gray souls to their final resting place. All were redeemed - their fear and pain and suffering were ended for eternity.

Lincoln, Grant and Lee knew nothing of this. No living soul knew anything of this. It was only for the assent of the concentration of so many departing souls. God had commanded the competing Archangels to work together on this mission.

David had been unconscious, lying on the ground, bleeding out and close to death before the medics had found him. In a dream he had a vision of what had occurred that night as he began to ascend and look down at his own body lying there on the ground with the thousands. He took in the whole of the event of the intervention by the holy third army - all the images, the lights in the black night - all at once and completely as a vivid reality.

He would not remember it later. Memory knows but knowing can't remember. For the rest of his life, he was troubled knowing there was evil, but wondering, not knowing, if there was goodness. Was it madness to know one and not the other? It was unresolved and he was unredeemed.

Seven - Andersonville

David woke up in the hospital and was recuperated briefly. He was taken to the overcrowded prison for Union captured in Richmond later that May. He was fortunate that gangrene had not set in and amputation of his leg was not necessary in his case. This was all too common in Civil War field medical practice.

But most often it was at the hospitals that the great piles of the limbs were amassed - the countless arms and legs. With the constant sounds of the wounded screaming, they were tossed into buckets to make it easier to cart them away and dump them into large holes in the ground.

As Grant continued his campaign, and the noose was tightening around Richmond, the security of the capital of the Confederacy was threatened. Because the prisoner exchange program had broken down, large numbers of Union prisoners were held there. The Confederacy hastily built a new prison in southwest Georgia at Andersonville.

It was intended to hold 10,000 Union prisoners. It was not as one would imagine a prison. There were no blockhouses around the perimeter. It was a stockade with 20 foot high log walls around an open field with a creek running through the middle of it. It grew to 26 acres. It operated from February 1864 until the end of the war in April 1865. Over 30,000 men were crowded onto the grounds and lived unsheltered in the open.

David was brought by railroad to the depot in the small village of Andersonville in July of 1864 with a group transported from Richmond. They were marched the quarter mile to the prison camp officially called Ft. Sumter. When he entered the compound, he thought it looked like a biblical Old Testament living nightmare. There was a noise in the air from the hum of mosquitoes and flies.

He immediately understood the danger, as well as the destitution, in this microcosm of a cruel society.

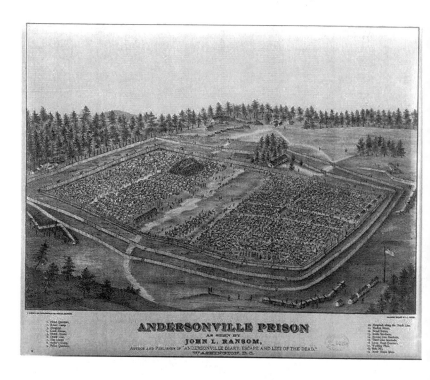

ANDERSONVILLE PRISON
AS SEEN BY
JOHN L. RANSOM,
AUTHOR AND PUBLISHER OF "ANDERSONVILLE DIARY, ESCAPE AND LIST OF THE DEAD."
WASHINGTON, D.C.

He found the prison camp a disarray of men held in the enclosure and living in the midst of slow dying and death. The men were ravaged by dysentery, scurvy and gangrene. There was insufficient food and the creek became an open sewer. Starvation, illness and disease brought death at a rate up to 100 per day.

The men were emaciated and their clothing was in tatters. The air was hot and fowl with human excrement. The ground was a slimy field of red clay muck with an odor of indescribable filth. It was covered with morsels of food and human feces and alive with maggots falling off festering wounds and grubs from rotting cornmeal.

There were some makeshift shelters made from blankets and remnants of uniforms hanging on wooden posts. The stream entering the camp under the stockade brought in human waste, cooking waste, and filthy water from the guards camp upstream. The scurvy became prevalent, and so painfully evident, when men sneezed out their teeth.

Groups of men had formed alliances to prey on weaker men and take from them anything they valued. They called themselves raiders, but they were predators. They were the worst threat to their own kind in the prison. And they were part of their own army.

Another group of men called themselves regulators and tried to protect the weak and bring a vigilante form of justice to this lawless, cruel society. Without care or concern from the guards, the regulators executed the worst of the raiders.

David soon joined the regulators and patrolled the compound the best he could with his slowly healing wounded leg. His strength and health were better than the many sick so close to death. His sense of justice compelled him to help the helpless.

He listened compassionately to his fallen comrades, sick and dying and fearful of attack from their own men. They told him about their families, so far away back home, and how long the war had lasted, far more than they had expected from the Confederates.

On one of his walks, he saw two men falling upon a one-armed man on the ground. They were pulling off his boots and snatching his blanket out from under him. The man's eyes were rimmed with red and sunken into deep sockets in his skull. His skin had the white pallor of death and his body was emaciated like a skeleton with the skin still on it.

David lunged at the man with the boots in his hands and smashed his fist into his jaw. As the man collapsed prone on the ground, David whirled around at the other man standing next to them.

He said, "How dare you? Have you no shred of human decency or compassion for your fellow man - your own comrade? God damn your empty soul and curse you for eternity."

Fleeting fear flashed through the man's eyes at David's ferocity, as he slowly backed away, turned and ran off.

David looked down at the ground in shock, and tears of anguish came to his eyes when he recognized the man was Patrick Allister. He sat by him for three days and talked to him about their times and great days in Baltimore. Patty didn't speak but answered with his eyes and expression that he had understood. They sat by the bank of the polluted stream with Pat's nearly lifeless body propped up against David's chest.

With silent tears streaming down his face, David said, "Oh Patty, what has become of you?" Patrick looked up into his eyes and smiled as his chest rose and heaved his last breath. As the air left his body with the last soft gasp of his last exhale, David saw the instant change to a stillness, different and more complete than any stillness at rest he had ever seen in a living person. Staring up at the incongruous beautiful blue sky, Patty was frozen in stillness forever more. This was just an empty shell of a body; his soul had departed.

David was conflicted with mixed feelings of sadness and anger. He couldn't fathom the anger. The rush of sadness overtook him, surprised him with its suddenness and its intensity. His heart leaped in his chest with a fullness of instant grief, like a fear or a shock.

After the throes of death had completed its course for both of them, David looked at Patrick's calm face and thought, 'What a price you have paid Patty. What a price we have all paid for this cause.'

There was a "dead line" understood to be several yards away from the stockade poles. Any prisoner who crossed it approaching the stockade walls was shot dead. There had been escape attempts - men digging tunnels under the log stockade. Many got out of Ft. Sumter but always were caught by the dogs and human trackers in a day or two.

Union officers imprisoned in the camp could not comprehend why Grant wouldn't exchange prisoners. Andersonville became a symbol of the whole country losing its humanity. The North held Confederates in a similar prison in urban Chicago - Ft. Douglas. However, that prison had barracks and the resources to provide better care for the prisoners. Ft. Douglas posed a dangerous threat to the citizens of Chicago however, and its presence was most unwelcome.

Seven

The whole South was starving and couldn't care for its northern prisoners. Yet Grant wouldn't agree to release his southern prisoners held in the North. He feared rehabilitating them would resupply the southern dwindling forces. Truly, many thought Grant's view of using his superior numbers to wear down the Confederate forces a cruel approach. But Lincoln agreed with him and it proved successful, while the losses were horrific for the Union.

Ultimately, Henry Wirz, the commandant of Andersonville, was brought to trial for his actions during his command of the camp. He was convicted of conspiracy and murder and hanged in Washington, DC on November 10, 1865.

David questioned Grant's sense of humanity and authority. He felt the abandonment and loneliness of his boyhood and questioned God's mercy. He could not understand why God gave men free will, while the Lord required giving themselves over to Him for the promise of salvation. He would search for understanding of God's grace and His plan for him and mankind for many years and write about these questions in his journal.

From his arrival in July to his release the following April, David was famished and became so malnourished, he lost 40 pounds from his 6 foot, 185 pound frame. He suffered from dysentery and grew so weak he nearly died. But he lived.

───────◦───────

Shortly after Lee's surrender, the prisoners were released and exchanged. The war was over. More than 650,000 Americans had given their lives and slavery was no more. The logic that drove the country to this solution was inexplicable, but in reality, the extent of it could not be expected or known beforehand. All the same, the nation had slipped into insanity. Slavery was barbaric but killing tens of thousands of men in a day was an awful price to pay to end it. Piles of humanity lay on the killing fields of Antietam and Shiloh. It was madness.

Many came to hope that future disputes could be solved with less passion and more patience. The country hoped for a return to normalcy and despaired for a time when men still believed they were creatures of God. Some had worn blue to preserve the Union and rid the country of slavery's evils. Other wore gray to preserve the homeland and defend against the tyranny of Federalism.

America's second revolution was lost; its Union preserved. The fight for independence from an oppressive government was finished. The fight for social justice had just begun. Perhaps even worse than the purgatory of the war itself was the real hell of the forced reconciliation. It took a lot longer. Foreign observers had believed we would never recover from its wounds.

President Lincoln's voice was stilled before his plans for forgiveness, and to heal the nation's wounds, could begin. Near the end of the war and his life, he had declared in his 2nd Inaugural Address that:

With malice toward none, with charity for all, with firmness in the right as God gives us to see the right, let us strive on to finish the work we are in, to bind up the nation's wounds, to care for him who shall have borne the battle and for his widow and his orphan, to do all which may achieve and cherish a just and lasting peace among ourselves and with all nations.

His vision was never to come to pass. The devastated South and its people would be in chaos and live with civil conflict and inhumanity for a century to come.

After his release from Andersonville, David decided to head west because he believed there he would find things new - places, opportunities, life. It was a rural and desolate two day walk from Andersonville to Columbus and the border with Alabama.

He was so weak and tired; he rested there and wrote his father:

Dearest Father;

I pray and trust that you are well. My deepest regret is that I have not been able to keep you informed of my war's journey and so much that has happened. I was wounded in Virginia near Richmond but survived my life's most horrible experience. I fail to find the sufficient words to express to you what I have experienced and seen.

The killing I saw and partook in will sicken my soul for the rest of my life. In the heat of it, there is no past, no future, only the moment. The mind crystallizes to a single pure focus as fear turns to hate and blood lust.

I was imprisoned in Georgia and lived through what this world would be like with no God to watch over it.

Seven

I saw Geoff Braxton's body carried away the day after the battle at Antietam. I held Patty Allister's wasted shell of a body and watched him heave his last breath at Andersonville prison. I know now man's original sin was not Adam and Eve; it was Cain and Abel.

At present, with the war over, I am traveling about the deep South in Georgia and will take a look at Alabama. I need to find some meaning in all this and won't be home for the foreseeable future.

Forgive me for that and know that I have always loved you for the greatest father that you are. I hope you will understand that I must do this. Whatever lessons I have been given, I must learn their meanings myself this time.

Your unconditional love for me, faith in me, and unfailing support for me has provided me strength to survive this trial.

Yr obt svt and devoted son,
David

He posted the letter in Columbus and began his search for himself and his life's meaning. His wounded leg and his crippled soul might never heal.

After crossing the Chattahooche River, he walked Alabama's bright red clay roads and passed through its eastern forested areas. It rained often in the spring. Some days there were brief showers with bright sunshine to follow, others a black sky with downpours for hours. The rain poured off the brim of his felt slouch hat. His sleeves were rolled up and his baggy pants were held up by suspenders over his thin frame. It soaked his shirt, his pants and his worn out shoes nearly through at the soles. The dry road turned to muck and the clay stuck to his shoes. His weak legs felt heavy.

He remembered the ground at Andersonville. It was miserable, but he had experienced it before in battle and in prison. It was bearable.

Along the way, he met some down-on-their-luck farmers who were kind enough to give him shelter and share what little they had to eat. He was grateful and paid for their kindness with his labor. Often they were badly in need of his carpentry skills. He was often invited to stay for a time and the respite helped him heal and gain strength.

He noted the simple lives of the plain folk and began writing about them in his journal. When he thought about it, David observed that it wasn't so much about what the South was, it was about what the North wasn't.

He thought, 'They speak of God and go to church more. They love their country. They love it more because they think about it as the land and their autonomy. It reminds me of Jefferson. He was a southerner, lifelong, from Virginia. I can see him back in those old times, playing his violin in his home - sweet southern sad melancholy American music from the earliest Colonial folk country tunes and Celtic heritage of those former days. It had the emotional tone of the old European classical folk music he loved too.'

Seven

He was repairing the broken porch steps on a farm house in Alabama when the farmer said to him, "Ya don't seem like a bad fella for a Yankee. Please come to service with us tomorra. We'd love to have ya."

The plain white folk had little to eat. But they had the land and they had the Lord. The church was full and the service was in the Baptist denomination - so prevalent in the South. He was raised a Presbyterian in Baltimore and attended services often with his father. But this was a different Christian worship. His had been warm and friendly, but dispassionate - with reassuring messages of salvation for believers.

This was full of passion and emotion. The people deeply felt the Holy Spirit. It pulled on their heartstrings; it made them smile; it made their eyes moist. It brought happiness to their hard-scrabble lives.

David watched them as they responded to the minister's powerful appeals. He sang with them the familiar hymns from his childhood. But he was surprised to see that in their tradition, with inadequate literacy, they did not use hymn books. They sang their familiar hymns from memory, learned from their oral tradition. They responded viscerally to the words of *What a Friend We Have in Jesus*.

As one, they swayed and looked heavenward to the soaring words and melody of *How Great Thou Art*:
Oh Lord my God, when I in awesome wonder
Consider all the worlds Thy hands have made,
I see the stars, I hear the rolling thunder,
Thy pow'r thro'out the universe displayed.

Then sings my soul, My Savior God, to Thee;

How great Thou art, how great Thou art!
Then sings my soul, My Savior God, to Thee;
How great Thou art, how great Thou art!

David would remember this. The power within those walls filled all its space and all the senses of the souls within. He had never witnessed or known of anything like this before. Perhaps the presence of God had actually been summoned forth.

He was deeply touched for them and the power of their faith. He felt it too, but couldn't cross over and make the commitment. He knew there was a Divine Providence - God's plan not revealed to him. He believed God intended for him to live by his free will and not to submit to authority, whether kind or cruel, whether Heavenly or of this earth.

He wrote in his journal on April 17th-
   Their faith brings so much to their lives. It is
   their light and their anchor. I wish I could see it
   and feel it as they do.

David spent the rest of April and most of May in Alabama but didn't find anything there to keep him from going further west. Others were wandering in this way too. He met many groups of Negroes looking for farm work, or some lost family members, or the chance to put down roots on land of their own.

This was the Deep South in the aftermath of slavery and war - searching for something better while surviving the best it could.

Eight - Meeting in Natchez

After wandering west across the South for many weeks, David came to the port of Natchez in Mississippi. He walked along the wharves and docks and looked out at the wide river. He remembered his days in the merchant marines and his voyages departing from Baltimore.

For him, there was something appealing about the South. He had fought in battles in Maryland and all over Virginia and watched so many of his countrymen die. He had been imprisoned in an outdoor sewer in Georgia. He hated the plantation aristocracy and slaveholders for the men that they were. He felt a kinship for the plain folk. So many of them were Scots-Irish.

But he had a feeling about the South that was difficult for him to understand. There was a prevailing sadness, yet he was attracted to it. Perhaps it had to do with his feeling of abandonment from the loss of his mother when she had died. He had grown up with aloneness and restless loneliness. It had been something he was used to.

This sadness might have been his warm companion he drew comfort from. And here in the South, it was something like a peaceful, bittersweet nostalgia as though he had lived here in a former life, in its rural country, before the war. It was melancholy and inexplicable.

David noticed a man staring out at the river. He was very still, deep in concentration. Well past mid-day, the man was cloaked in the shadow of the waterfront buildings. He stood at a distance watching him and sensed a sadness and loneliness - an aloneness - about him that he could understand well. There were several people in the area but no one nearby but he and this man.

He felt compelled to walk over to greet him and speak to him. He now saw that the man was a Negro. He noticed a strong resolve and sense of purpose in the man's eyes and wasn't certain how he would be received. He was curious and decided to speak to him.

David approached the man in a casual, friendly and cheerful manner and said, "Hello, my name is David, who are you?"

Josiah was startled by this stranger and his question. He was not sure if this man was a threat. Most white men he had known in his life had treated him harshly. For the most part, they could not be trusted. With hesitancy, he thought it best to reply and avoid trouble.

So he answered, "My name is Josiah, suh."

David immediately realized that the man was wary, possibly afraid, and continued, "I mean you no harm. I just wondered what you were doing here, looking at the river I mean."

Josiah looked at him closely and thought he sensed a sadness and loneliness in this friendly white man.

He hesitated for a moment and said, "I am a freed man from a plantation near here. I came here hoping to find what to do next and mostly to look for my lost wife."

"Well I guess we have more in common than we would expect meeting here like this", David said. "I have just been freed from a prison in Georgia and have walked across

Alabama to come to Mississippi searching for what I will do next."

Josiah nodded and the two men continued to assess each other for a few minutes. Josiah was surprised to be approached like this by a white man. David had fought to end the inhumanity and injustice of slavery, had always known it was a sinful abomination, but had never met a former slave to talk to before this.

The two men sensed, and began to understand, some shared commonness and both thought there might be a possibility for friendship even though their skin color was not the same and there was no true trust yet established. Despite their initial wariness as strangers, they spent the afternoon talking to each other about their life's fortunes and hopes for the future.

The afternoon turned to dusk and with nightfall approaching, David asked, "Have you eaten today?"

Josiah replied, "I have been here two days and met some people on the dock. I helped them unload a ship's cargo. They gave me some food, a blanket and a place to sleep in that warehouse over there. It felt a little strange but good to work for myself, earn my keep and keep what I earn for my own benefit as a free man."

David said, "Well, I have met many strangers on my travels here too. Most of them were poor farmers who suffered damage and destruction during the war. I helped them repair some farm buildings and equipment and I baled some cotton. Like you, as payment for my labor, they fed me and gave me a place to sleep in their barns."

Eight

As darkness set in on the river's edge, the men talked more about their situation and future hopes.

Josiah wondered if this could be the start of a friendship with this white man from the North, but was uncertain how to act on an equal basis and careful not to offend him.

Hesitantly he said, "David, you can sleep at the warehouse tonight it you want. It is not very comfortable like a house."

David laughed and replied, "No, no don't worry about it. It will be fine. After my imprisonment in Georgia, I am not particular about where I sleep."

Together they left the waterfront for the night. As they walked toward the warehouse, Josiah noticed that his new companion was very thin and walked with a limp from his left leg.

The next morning they talked more comfortably about their concerns, hopes and plans. As they shared their past, Josiah described some of his life as a slave. He discovered that David was a very educated and knowledgeable man. Josiah thought that maybe David would be able to give him some answers to questions that had troubled him for years. David would learn that Josiah was a serious minded, purposeful man.

With his expression formed with resolve, Josiah asked, "David, how did you think we became slaves? I mean I know we were brought from Africa, but how and why did it start?"

David thoughtfully replied, "It's a long story Josiah. My grandfather used to tell me how our country began when the early English settlers came to Virginia. They believed they were noblemen like back in England. Slavery began then over 250 years ago when African slaves were brought to Virginia from the Caribbean. There was a trade going on between England, West Africa, the Caribbean and our colonies. Slaves were traded for tobacco, rum, sugar and molasses. Everybody was making a lot of money on the human traffic."

Josiah remarked, "The old slaves on the plantations told me that we used to be up in Virginia and Carolina. We planted tobacco. Life was not as hard then as it is now here in the Deep South. Massa Taylor never talked about it. He just said we are just cotton pickin' niggers and we have to work hard or we will be lashed."

David said, "Yes I know. That word, and the word Negroes, came from ancient Latin and was a word from back in Africa meaning people of black skin color. The plantation owners are ignorant southerners and were just trying to control you."

His fists were balled up when he said, "I hate the godless, evil, aristocratic bastards."

They were both quiet and reflective for a few minutes after that emotional outburst. Josiah was startled by David's feelings of rage. He didn't yet know David's nature when confronted with matters of injustice and cruel authority. He tried to take in everything David had told him and the sense it was given.

With calm restored, their talk moved on to their very different past lives and their skills. They began to speak to each other about their ideas for the future.

Josiah remarked, "David I understand I am free now and I own myself for the first time. I don't know what to do next to find work or how to begin to look for Josie."

David answered, "I understand what you mean. I started out in Baltimore. For a few years, I sailed ships as a Merchant Marine. What stories I could tell you about those experiences. I am a Yankee and I fought for the Union and Lincoln in Virginia. I was shot in the leg, captured and taken prisoner over to Georgia to the prison in Andersonville. When the war ended, I was released and I traveled around the South looking for a place for myself. I ended up here in Natchez just as you have."

Josiah listened and then asked, "What will you do now?"

David thought and replied slowly, "I'm not sure Josiah but I need to find a place where I can be free to work and live, just like you. Even though Baltimore is my home, I didn't feel happy living in the city. I could never have worked in a factory for wages or any other job for long where I was under the authority of others. When I left the Merchant Marines, I began to hire myself out to do carpentry. I built houses and other things, learning and using my skills as I went along."

Josiah agreed, "Yes I am similar. I learned how to build furniture. Woodworking is different than carpentry. It takes a long time to build a chair or a table. I learned carpentry from an older craftsman on the plantation. Slowly I found that I had skills and understood the figures and grains of good woods. You need to know how to shape and smooth the wood and finish the pieces with stains and linseed oil. It takes patience but the finished work makes me proud. It is slow but I really enjoy it."

David told him, "I can appreciate the beautiful things that you can make. But, for myself, I work much faster and work with rough wood and don't worry about the beautiful finishes. But I can throw up a strong house frame in two to three days. Maybe we can go together to find work and look for your Josie."

Josiah was touched and pleased that a man he had just met would throw in with him and be his companion and ally, "Yes, that would be a great comfort to have us travel together. In these dangerous times, two are stronger than one. I'm sure there will be times when trouble will come. By the way, my last name is Ashford, the name of my first owner in Missouri."

"Well it's a pleasure Mr. Ashford. Mine is Wexley from Baltimore. If you don't mind me asking, I couldn't help noticing how well spoken and serious minded you are. Have you read or studied? I thought slaves were not allowed to read or write."

"It's funny you asked that. You are right. Most slaves are forbidden to learn to read. My Josie worked in the mansion and sneaked books to our cabin when she came at night. I taught myself to read. I read some of the good ones."

He laughed to himself and said, "Your experience as a sailor in the Merchant Marines made me remember *Moby Dick*."

"Ha ha. I read that one too. I never fought an epic battle with a whale, but did fire some cannon at British ships."

Josiah and David had begun to form a bond forged from a common experience. They had witnessed the face of inhumanity in its most horrible expression. They were both burdened with survivor's guilt. This shared life experience was similar enough that it transcended any differences they may have had. The strength of their bond would protect them in the many difficult days ahead.

David understood better his conflicted feelings about the South and its appeal. It wasn't just about the places. It was about some of its people. It brought him a measure of happiness - something he had always searched for.

Nine - Rise and Fall of Savannah Oaks

The early years, starting in late 1835, were filled with back breaking work and ceaseless activity as Marcus built the plantation on his swamp timber land. He had purchased six field hands, a carpenter, a blacksmith, and a house servant girl at the slave auction in Natchez to get started. One of those field hands was the female named Sarah.

After two years, most of the work was completed to start the plantation operation. The first planting was started on 95 acres of his land. The cottonseed was in and work had begun on the mansion. The network of dirt roads had been established for entrance to the main house and access to the slave cabins and work fields. Funds were depleting from Hendrick's investment in his son's new business.

Marcus had made remarkable progress. By 1838, he was ready for and had procured the 50 slaves he needed to support his cotton production on 525 of his 650 acres. The rest would remain unused open or forested land. The main house was completed and Marcus and Rebecca moved out of their crude temporary house.

Rebecca was pleased to move into her mansion and settle the fine household she had waited for. She learned how to manage and direct her staff of Negro attendants. Marcus left her to her role since he was completely immersed in his. He was determined to make a success of the plantation and keep his promises to Rebecca and his father.

Hendrick made the trip to visit them shortly after that.

He looked the plantation over and told Marcus, "You have done well son."

He thought to himself, 'Even with its refinements, I wouldn't want to live in a place like this. There's nothing can be done about its rural crudeness.'

Marcus thought his father looked much older and less enthusiastic about his life.

Between the planting and harvesting seasons, he and Rebecca made the trip to Savannah to visit him. They gathered the family together. Jane was not well, but still alive and living with Hendrick in their home. Marcy and Constance and their families came to join them.

The Taylors held a party so that all the Stanleys could come down from Charleston. Rebecca was so happy to see them all again. She had missed her family and her brothers in particular. She had been very close to them from all the time they spent traveling together. But things seemed different now. Everyone was older and had gone on with their lives.

She thought, 'I guess there is no going back.'

She decided to make the best of it at Savannah Oaks. She began an effort to build a social structure with the neighbors in two of the nearby plantations. She planned and carried out many successful parties as she had known in the past.

But the scale was not as grand and the people were more concerned about their cotton and the control of their slaves than the social graces. This rural life would never be the same as she knew in the earlier days in Charleston or Savannah. But there was no going back.

Marcus and Rebecca had surely changed - they were slaveholders now. The Negroes were a means to their end. Their human property was the same as their other non-human property and equipment. The immorality of this became suppressed until it was forgotten.

They were morally corrupt and inhumane but viewed themselves as paternal and maternal benefactors caring for their inferior children. Their children were well cared for, but when they misbehaved, punishment was meted out with harsh brutality.

By 1843, Savannah Oaks had prospered better then Marcus had ever hoped for. He had 160 slaves and had brought his cash crops to market in Natchez for many seasons. The household was splendid and alive under Rebecca's management. There were cooks, seamstresses, housekeepers and servants looking after all her needs at the mansion. Noticeably missing were nursemaids since Marcus and Rebecca had never had children.

In 1852, Marcus bought Josiah and brought him to the plantation as a prime, 23 year old field hand with potential as a fair hand at carpentry. Josena was 15 years old and working in the house as a servant. Josiah fell in love with Josena and married her in 1853.

Marcus had fought with Rebecca for years over Josena. Rebecca had been unable to conceive and remained childless. She knew Marcus was Josena's father. He had no choice but to acknowledge that fact and care for his daughter. As Josena grew up over the passing years, Rebecca's resentment grew. Even when Josena married Josiah, Rebecca would never let Marcus forget his disloyalty to her.

Finally the pressure convinced him to sell her. He found a way to do so, and in February 1856, he secretly sold her in Natchez. He brought her by wagon and she never came back.

Josiah was up at the saw mill away from the main house and road that day. When he returned and Josena didn't come home from the mansion, he was beside himself with worry and didn't know what to do. His first thought was to go to Marcus and ask where she was but he knew that was not wise. He frantically asked everyone he saw if anyone had seen her or knew her whereabouts. Two of the slaves told him they saw her go off with Massa Marcus early that morning in the back of his wagon. The Massa came back with an empty wagon. They all knew what that meant.

Josiah went to Ned's cabin. He was angry, distraught, desperate and frightened.

He thought, 'This can't be true. Where is she?'

Sobbing so hard his throat would barely let him croak, "Ned, what has happened to Josie?"

Ned confirmed what he had heard about Marcus selling Josie.

Josiah hung his head and sobbed, "How could he sell his daughter? What should I do, Ned? I don't know how to go on without her."

Ned tried to console him as best he could, said, "Yo can't face up ta Massa, Josiah. Yo mus 'cept dis and go on with yo life. We neva understan da cruelty of a man like dat Massa. Yo mus let yo faith in Jesus hep yo go on. Josie wouldn't want anythin' to happen to yo; yo knows dat."

Josiah told him, "I don't think I can go back to our cabin. Everywhere I look there is a reminder of her. What am I going to do?"

Ned offered, "Come stay with me, boy. Leas' fo tonight. In the mornin' we kin think 'bout what we do tomorra."

So Josiah stayed with Ned and, after a few days, moved his meager belongings and a few treasured books that he had kept when no one at the mansion missed them, into Ned's cabin. Life went on in the slave quarters, as it had before, without Josena, just as though she had never existed.

Josiah grieved for her absence and wondered if she was still alive. He poured himself into his work and bided his time. On some bright clear days, his hands slowed down and fell to his side as he stared at the wood he was fashioning. He looked out across the cotton fields at the sad live oaks, draped in moss, lining the road leading away and wondered.

———————◦———————

By July 1863 Grant had won the siege of Vicksburg and the Mississippi River was under the control of the Union. Grant had left the west to participate in campaigns in Virginia, but some Union forces remained behind to maintain control of the Mississippi Valley area.

For Marcus Taylor, this meant he could no longer access Natchez for selling his cotton or for trading in slavery. His slaves were theoretically freed, but no federal forces had entered his plantation.

When Marcus learned about the occupation of the federal troops in Natchez and Lincoln's emancipation of the slaves, he became very concerned for his plantation and his way of life. He knew it was only a matter of time until they discovered his remote plantation. He feared that the Union forces would emancipate his slaves and possibly burn his plantation.

While he and Rebecca no longer felt any love between them, they still shared a bond as master and mistress of Savannah Oaks. They were still partners in their life's business and livelihood. Marcus talked to her about his worries.

He said, "Rebecca, the Yankees have now occupied Natchez. We are in deep trouble. We can't bring our crops to market or buy or sell any slaves with them there."

"Can't we bribe some officials and get around them if only to sell our cotton?"

Marcus looked resigned and said, "No, we will get caught and then they will come here and find us."

Rebecca had a thought and suggested, "Maybe we will have to put more work into our vegetable garden and have our coloreds do the same for theirs. The men will have to spend their time hunting for game. We will have to live off the land until we see how this ends."

It ended when the federal troops arrived at Savannah Oaks in July of 1865. By then, the plantation had seen its better days. After nearly two years without income from cotton production, Marcus had let many of his slaves wander away. He had no means to support them. And his attitude and treatment of them had changed under the new circumstances. He had come to realize that his control over them was weakening while perhaps he and Rebecca were more dependent on them than before.

Some had stayed for lack of a better alternative until the authorities arrived and forced the decision. Particularly the older slaves stayed since they were more dependent on their owners for their welfare. But they were not as useful as the younger ones who had left.

Marcus and Rebecca survived the best they could, subsisting on Savannah Oaks plantation.

Josiah quietly kept to himself and stayed because he had become a respected craftsman and was treated better than most. The slaves looked up to him, often came to him to seek advice and accepted him as a leader. They were respectful of his loss.

He continued to try to improve himself and find his faith. He reread the books he had kept. He practicing reading them aloud to hear the sound the words made with his voice. His favorite was Harriet Beecher Stowe's *Uncle Tom's cabin, or, Life among the lowly*. It was Rebecca's but she had not missed it and likely not read it.

Alone at the saw mill he spoke out with emotion and passion:

A day of grace is held out to us. Both North and South have been guilty before God; and the Christian church has a heavy account to answer. Not by combining together, to protect injustice and cruelty, and making a common capital of sin, is this Union to be saved, - but by repentance, justice and mercy; for, not surer is the eternal law by which the millstone sinks in the ocean, than the stronger law, by which injustice and cruelty shall bring on nations the wrath of Almighty God!

It had been nine years since Massa Taylor had sold Josena. He had been bitter and angry about losing her for a long time. He wondered again and again, 'How could a father sell his daughter?' No one had come into his life to replace her, nor would he want that. He drifted along and found gratification in his work.

When word came about the emancipation of slaves in Confederate controlled territories, he was still conflicted about what to do about it. He didn't see any way to do anything at that time. So he waited until the officials came and declared him free. He never gave up hope that he would find Josena again someday.

The year was 1865. The bright sun in the southern sky had faded by late afternoon in the late spring - past its former glory, never forgotten, but gone forever.

At the end of the war, Savannah Oaks became a sharecropper farm, with freedmen as labor, under the new post-war reconstruction arrangements. Their slaves had all left and their land was sub-divided into small plots for the new farmers - Negro strangers - to manage. Marcus and Rebecca moved to a small plot near the place where the new town of McComb was being built.

With their human property gone, they had lost most of their wealth. They sold off their land for what little they could get and kept a small plot of 20 acres for themselves. Marcus worked the land as a small farmer and hired a couple Negroes to help him with the planting and harvesting. He had no place for them to live on his land. He paid them wages and they came in from their cabins on the other side of McComb.

They grew vegetables for themselves and some cotton to help pay for what they had to buy. He hunted small and large game in the woods and fields of Savannah Oaks on their former property. He cut wood and they survived the winters as the years passed away.

Rebecca kept the house and read her books about genteel people living their elegant lives in grand cities. They lived together as working partners and companions. They subsisted in that way too, since there had been no love between them for many years.

Finally Marcus's heart gave out at harvest time and she buried him in the cemetery in McComb in the fall of 1881. They had no rights for the use of the cemetery on the former Savannah Oaks plantation. After that, she lived by herself, never left the house, and retreated from the world more and more as time passed. She was a widow who had no grief for her husband but grieved for her own life throughout most of its remainder. That was, until she lost her mind.

The town folk passed by her house and saw her delicate frail hand holding back the lace curtain as she stared out of the window of her dark room. Each time they saw her, she never looked at them or knew they were there; her trace-like eyes were gazing at some other thing, some other place.

A Negress in town had been helping several white families keep house. She had come to Mississippi from Mobile, Alabama by herself to look for work. She did their laundries and was a nanny to their children. This black Christian woman gave their children love or a sharp tongue in just the best way it was needed. The white folk took exception to her color and loved her as the fine Christian woman she was.

She took mercy on the demented widow who lived by herself and began going to her house one day a week to help out in any way she could as an act of Christian charity. The Christian woman looked after the woman's needs and kept her company as her only companion. She patiently listened to the fantasies living in the old woman's mind.

Rebecca recounted her stories as she remembered them, not as they were in truth or knowing, "We had the finest plantation and the grandest mansion, just as Marcus had promised. We fed the brave Confederate soldiers that came through in our grand dining room with our best silver and services. The starving and famished men were served our most lavish diners and our musicians played them the glorious music of our south in our grand ballroom.

But after a while the niggers began taking our fine things little by little. I never could catch them but you can never trust niggers. Soon everything was gone and soon Marcus was gone. I look out the window for him."

Nine

The Negress companion listened patiently week after week to the old woman, sitting with her in the small dark living room with only the afternoon light coming through the lace curtains of the windows. She watched this woman in her dirty frayed dress, the same she wore each week. She saw that her mind had slipped its moorings - she was hopelessly insane.

She comforted her, "Now, now ol girl, yo kin always rely on de Lord. He make it right."

When Rebecca died in 1888, the Christian colored woman arranged Rebecca's pauper's funeral and the burial service in the McComb town cemetery. A few town folks came, more for curiosity than care. The woman had been the last person to speak to Rebecca and now was the last one to speak about her.

She prayed, "Oh Jesus, sweet Jesus, take dis wumun in yo eva luvin arms. Keep her soul in hevin with yo for all eternity. Amen."

She had come by herself from Mobile, Alabama to work for the white folk. She had never known her daddy but had heard her mamma's name was Josena.

Nine

Ten - Looking for Josie

Josiah and David were thinking about how to begin looking for Josena. Josiah suggested, "We should start here in Natchez. Let's talk to people who know about the slave auction and see what we can find out."

It didn't take long for them to find the market known as *The Forks of the Road*, the largest former slave auction, at the intersection of Liberty Road and Washington Road. The market was no longer in operation but a man there told them that all records of slave transactions had been confiscated by the federal government. They would need to go to the Freedmen's Bureau.

Josiah looked at David and said "We will have to go to the plantation and get Marcus Taylor to show us his records."

David was more than ready to confront Taylor and get the records of sale, even if he had to beat it out of him. And so they decided to begin their trek by first going back to Savannah Oaks.

They found Marcus there as a disheveled, beaten and defeated man. He had no fighting spirit left in him.

Josiah told him, "We need to see your records of sales for slaves you sold. We are looking for my wife, Josena that you sold away from me."

Marcus looked crestfallen - she was his daughter - and said, "I remember."

Ten

It was one of the most shameful acts he had ever committed, and one of the most regrettable.

He looked through his papers in his office of the plantation main house and produced a bill of sale. It was dated February 13, 1856 and stated that a John Manford from Alabama had purchased one Josena Taylor as an 18 year old house servant for $850. There was no location or plantation name for the buyer.

David said, "C'mon let's go. There's nothing more for us here."

Marcus said, "Before you go, stay for a good meal. You're welcome to stay here tonight and get a fresh start in the morning."

Josiah said, "We will take you up on your offer for a meal."

Marcus led them through the grand foyer to the servants' big kitchen at the back of the house. He instructed his cook to serve them a meal. They ate a good portion of crawfish, jambalaya, and fresh cornbread. As they got up to leave the kitchen, Josiah remembered building the large table there. He had made it several years ago from Southern pecan hardwood, milled on the plantation property. He was pleased to see how durable it had been.

Marcus joined them again as they walked out the grand front door of the plantation main house onto the veranda. Rebecca was sitting in her rocker on the porch but didn't look over at them.

Ten

She was staring off towards the fields, fallow now for these last few years. All the memories had come flooding back to her. She remembered the heady days of her youth in Charleston - the parties, the attention, the refinement- and the energy and excitement of Savannah. She remembered the broken promises for a life like that here. She remembered the years that Josena had been raised in the main house and had served there. Most of all, she remembered the supreme act of disloyalty by her husband. With no children of her own and living in this remote place, she had wasted all her best years. She despaired for what a disappointment her life had been.

When she heard the voices and the shuffling feet on the porch, she awoke from her bitter reverie, looked up and said to Josiah, "So you are looking for that young Negro woman are you? Good riddance to her and her kind."

Josiah was startled by her venom but responded, "I'm not looking for your opinions and won't concern myself with how I address you. I won't refer to you as my Owner, my Mistress, or my Massa's wife. I am a free man now. Goodnight Rebecca."

David and Josiah filled their canteens with fresh water from the pump in the front yard. Josiah looked back at the main house and across the side yard at the slave cabins. He remembered his 13 years here in human bondage. There were some pleasant memories. He had made friends and allies and was respected for his artisanship.

Most of all, he remembered Josena, the love they had between them, and their brief two-year marriage before she was taken away. He knew that much had changed in just a few weeks since he had left the plantation.

He envisioned much more change to come. His people would never again be treated like farm animals and beasts of burden and inferior human beings. There would be many good and bad white people and black people involved in the change that would occur over many, many years. He knew also that there would be special relationships, formed from some common bonds, between black people and white people - like he and David.

But he knew that, in the end, his people would have the opportunity for an equal share in American citizenship. People of African descent would always consider themselves as unique and different because of their history as victims of the "peculiar institution". They had been slaves and had become freedmen. Because of their history of slavery, they would come to view themselves as African-Americans apart from white Americans. They would develop a pride that white people would not understand.

David broke into Josiah's reverie and said, "Let's get started. We have a couple more hours of daylight. I don't want to stay here tonight."

They started out together walking down the old road away from the plantation. It was another hot and humid July night in Mississippi. They would sleep in the fields and start out on their journey again tomorrow.

The next morning David suggested, "Since our answers might be found in Alabama, I think we should go to Mobile. I passed through there on my way to Natchez a couple months ago. It is a growing city and port to the Gulf. Maybe we can meet someone who will give us useful information to look for Josie."

The trip to Mobile was nearly 300 miles and took them the rest of July and most of August. They met many small groups of freedmen wandering from town to town. Planters, small farmers, and town's people viewed them with suspicion and there was always the threat of violence. They stopped in several places and traded their carpentry skills for food, shelter and provisions. They carried blanket rolls and gunnysacks necessary for travel on the road. Recognizing the potential for personal danger, David bought two old army .44-cal. Model 1860 Colt revolvers, holsters and ammunition. He taught Josiah to handle and shoot his if the need for self-defense arose.

Life was changing dramatically and rapidly in the Deep South. In 1865, Mississippi and Alabama had not rejoined the Union. Radical Republicans in the federal government had many ideas to experiment with the transformation of the post-war southern society and economy. Federal troops were stationed in regions of the South to impose martial law and maintain order. Whites were struggling to find ways to recoup their way of life. Blacks were struggling to find new ways to live as free men. The tension between them was palpable.

When they arrived at the port of Mobile, they found it occupied by federal troops and under martial law. In August 1864, the naval siege of Mobile had concluded with the fall of Fort Morgan. The Union army had also participated in the defeat of the Confederates there. The port was closed and blockaded.

David spoke to a federal officer at the town office center. He asked him if anyone kept any records with information about the whereabouts of an Alabama man named John Manford. He explained they were trying to locate him and it was believed he was a slave owner and likely had a plantation.

The officer said, "I don't know anyone here who would have kept records to help you locate him. I suggest you go to Demopolis about 150 miles north of here. Negroes had been excluded from that town as slaves before the war, but now the Freedmen's Bureau has a regional office there to assist them with relocation and finding family members."

David thanked him and looked over at Josiah and said, "Well Joe, that sounds like our next stop."

Josiah smiled and in a rare lighthearted moment, said, "Let's go Dave."

They found Demopolis to be a very small town crowded with freedmen milling about and looking hopeful that there would be assistance. They waited in line at the Freedmen's Bureau office for their turn.

Joe told the agent that they needed to find a slave named Josena Taylor. She was his wife and had been sold to a John Manford at the slave auction in Natchez on February 13, 1856. They believed he had a plantation in Alabama.

The agent said, "I'm closing in a half hour but if you will come back tomorrow morning, I'll let you know what I found out."

That evening they talked to several freedmen in the town and learned that they were all on a similar quest and were hanging onto hope. The next morning, they met the agent again.

He smiled and said "I have some good news for you. There is a John Manford who works as an overseer and agent for the

Drish Plantation in Tuscaloosa. They are a major cotton producer in this region. Just now, many of their slaves have left and they are making the transition to sharecropping. Manford conducted a lot of business for John Drish and did buy a slave named Josena for him at the Natchez auction in 1856. They are located about 60 miles north of here."

Joe was excited and said to David "That's it. We will go to the Drish Plantation and get Josena."

Joe and David traveled north toward Tennessee and found Tuscaloosa and the Drish Plantation in west central Alabama a week after leaving Demopolis. They had followed along the Black Warrior River which flowed south to the Gulf at Mobile.

The area was located on the boundary between the Appalachian Highland and the Gulf Coastal Plain. The geography was diverse with heavily forested hills and low-lying marshy plains. The climate in summer was warm and the air was moist. Severe seasonal thunderstorms and tornadoes were common this time of year.

The new city nearby lie on the fall line upriver from the confluence with the Tombigbee River at Demopolis. During the last weeks of the war, Union troops had raided the area and burned the town and new college there.

John Drish was a physician from Virginia who settled near Tuscaloosa in 1822. He built his plantation in 1835 on a 450 acre plot of land. He ran a large cotton mill operation there with his slaves and, as an amateur architect, cultivated them as skilled artisans in carpentry, masonry and plasterwork.

Drish had completed his stuccoed brick mansion in 1837 and had it built in the Greek and Italianade styles unique to the area. It had full width Doric porticoes to the front and rear with two-story pilasters dividing the bays on four sides. He helped design the mansion himself and had it built by his slave artisans.

A three-story brick tower was added before the war. There was an oak tree lined entrance road leading up to the mansion from where there was a view of the Black Warrior River.

John Manford was the overseer for the Drish Plantation operations. He was standing in front of the mansion portico and watching the two men walking up the road approaching him. He briefly glanced over at his shotgun and hollered toward them, "What brings you fellas round here on foot this hot afternoon?"

They met him in the yard at the end of the entrance road. His shirt sleeves were rolled up and he wore suspenders to hold up his work pants. His wide brimmed straw hat shaded his round face and mutton chop sideburns.

They could tell he had been hard muscled once but was drifting toward sloppy fat in his late middle age. He was a short man who appeared affable and wore a sardonic smile. His friendly appearance was deceptive when Joe and David considered Manford's position.

They explained their purpose to Manford and Joe asked him if Josena was still here. The smile faded from Manford's face and he said, "Yes, she is here."

Eleven - After Bondage and War

On April 9th, with General Lee's meager forces surrounded in the Village of Appomattox Court House by the overwhelming forces of Grant's generals, and with all escape routes blocked, he decided to end the fight. When Sheridan saw Lee's defenseless forces huddled together, he asked Grant to permit him to ignore the fragile cease fire and for the order to annihilate them. He said it would only take five minutes.

Grant angrily told him, "No, that would place our names in infamy forever."

Lee waited in the home of Wilmer McLean for Grant's arrival. They met to discuss the terms of surrender as gentlemen and with dignity. They drafted brief documents and, through their attendants, exchanged them. Lee's final letter addressed Grant as commander of all the armies of the United States, including his own, and awaited his orders.

Grant would have nothing of Lee surrendering his sword. That would have brought no honor to the ceremony and would have only served the newspapers and politicians.

He remembered the words in the Old Testament of the Holy Book, and thought, 'The prophet Micah reminds us: *He has showed you, O man, what is Good. And what does the Lord require of you? To act justly and to love mercy and walk humbly with your God.*'

He paroled the men and permitted them to leave and go back to their homes. He required they surrender and stack up their arms and ammunition. Officers were permitted to keep their side arms. All cavalry soldiers could take their personal horses and mules back to their farms. The terms were as generous as Lee could have hoped for.

Grant ordered Sheridan, "Provide food rations to the beaten Confederates. They have been starved for many months. Take care of them. That is my order. See to it." Sheridan obeyed.

Across the fields, a spontaneous celebration of cannon and musket fire broke out from the Union forces. Grant ordered it to cease immediately.

He expressed his belief, "There is no dignity or honor in humiliation. The enemy knows full well they are beaten. The Confederates are now our countrymen."

Both Lee and Grant knew that there was no glory in war, but there was dignity and respect between its combatants. For war's leaders, the purpose was to inspire men to march and face the enemy across the killing field - to fight for their country. They were trained to believe that and had lived their whole lives with that code. They had learned the meaning of duty and that guided all their actions and conduct. They understood the meaning of honor better than others ever would.

After Lee's farewell address to his army on April 10th, Union Brigadier General Joshua L. Chamberlain was charged with leading the ceremony for the formal surrender on April 12th. Chamberlain reflected on what he had observed and wrote a moving tribute containing these words:

Before us in proud humiliation stood the embodiment of manhood: men whom neither toils and sufferings, nor the fact of death, nor disaster, nor hopelessness could bend from their resolve; standing before us now, thin, worn, and famished, but erect, and with eyes looking level into ours, waking memories that bound us together as no other bond;—was not such manhood to be welcomed back into a Union so tested and assured? Instructions had been given; and when the head of each division column comes opposite our group, our bugle sounds the signal and instantly our whole line from right to left, regiment by regiment in succession, gives the soldier's salutation, from the "order arms" to the old "carry"—the marching salute. Gordon at the head of the column, riding with heavy spirit and downcast face, catches the sound of shifting arms, looks up, and, taking the meaning, wheels superbly, making with himself and his horse one uplifted figure, with profound salutation as he drops the point of his sword to the boot toe; then facing to his own command, gives word for his successive brigades to pass us with the same position of the manual,—honor answering honor.

No expression could have captured the common bond of esprit de corps for the soldiers of the North and South better than this.

———————————◦◦◦———————————

After the war, the economic order of the old South was destroyed. For its people, like their many deserted battlefields, the economic playing field was leveled. In an ironic way, there was more economic equality. The many white poor remained desperately poor as before. The many freedmen became poor by virtue of their independence. The few and powerful rich whites became more poor with their system, based on enslaved labor, removed. All their human property had been taken from them. New alternatives would be required to rebuild their system. Without a significant industrial economy, the South would first need to invent a new agricultural system. Industrialization and the new South would come much later.

The social order was also destroyed. With their way of life gone forever and their cause lost, the defeated white southerners were consumed with bitterness toward the North and its victorious government. For the first time in their lives, the freedmen would need to find their rightful place in society.

Hatred, resentment, and even jealousy would be turned in their direction by the embittered whites. As a new reality, the freedmen would need to be dealt with by all of society. A century of racism and violence would follow before these matters were settled in law.

———————————————

For Josiah and David, their journey was over. They had found the Drish Plantation in Tuscaloosa, Alabama and met John Manford. He had told them Josena was there.

Joe said to Manford, "Please, please take me to her."

He led them to an area in the field behind the plantation main house. It was surrounded by a wrought iron fence. He led them through the gate to a simple stone marker that was inscribed "Josena- Beloved House Girl - Died September 1864". Josiah stood before the grave and fell to his knees.

He wailed in anguish, "God, how could you do this? I can't believe this has happened."

Josiah sobbed bitterly and couldn't quell the tears running down his face. David stood beside him speechless with his hand on Josiah's shoulder.

Eleven

David asked John Manford what had happened. He learned that there had been a slave uprising as word came that Union forces had seized Mobile and were occupying Alabama. The plantation slaves had charged the overseers with shovels, pitchforks, and clubs. There were shots fired and the rebellion intensified. The confrontation got out of control and several slaves were killed. Josena had been in the yard on an errand for the main house and was accidentally shot in the abdomen. She could not be saved and died two hours later.

When Josena had been bought and brought to Drish Plantation, she was three-months pregnant with Josiah's child. John Drish was a kindly man and always treated her well as part of his household servant staff. When he saw that she was going to have a baby, he was gentle and supportive. His wife took a special interest in her and, for the first time in her life, the mistress of the plantation had shown her mercy and human kindness.

Manford paid no attention to the household relationships or matters within the mansion. His work running the operations of the plantation filled his time and interest.

But Josena never stopped grieving for her separation from Josiah and remained despondent for the rest of her life.

Like the mythic, long-wandering journey to come home and find her, Odysseus, embodied in two men - the seeker and the wanderer - had found Penelope. But she hadn't been waiting faithfully, surrounded by duplicity; she had been killed too soon. This war, and its human stories, had ended in tragedy and heartbreak, not joy.

Manford said, "It was a tragedy. We all loved Josena. It broke the hearts of all of us - the Negroes and us alike."

David pulled Manford aside and left Joe alone at the gravesite.

Manford said, "Three days after the incident, the Yankee troops arrived and said our Negroes was freed. It was such a waste; four Negroes and Josena dead. There was Freedmen's Bureau government people who explained we could make contracts with our Negroes so they could work as sharecroppers. Many of them left anyway. We have been trying to convert the plantation since then. The Negroes didn't know how good they had it when we took care of them."

David looked at him steely eyed and said, "They didn't know how good they had it? You mean they were better off when they were whipped for looking at you the wrong way or speaking the wrong word. They were better off when they couldn't leave the plantation without your permission, or when you sold off their husbands, wives or children. They were better off when you raped their women. They were better off working for you from dawn to dusk in a gang until they died young before their time."

Manford said, "Well, what's done is done. You boys can stay for a couple days if Joe needs some time. I'll ask John Drish to have the servants prepare some rooms for you."

David responded, "If it's all the same to you, we'll stay in the barn with the horses tonight. I prefer the company."

Manford snuffed, "As you wish."

As he began to walk away, he looked back at David and said, "I forgot to tell ya. When Josena come here, she was light with child. We didn't know it 'til a few months later when she had a little picaninny girl. After Josena was kilt, John Drish sold the child off to a gentleman in Mobile as a house servant."

David decided that this would be too much to tell Joe right then, so he kept it to himself.

That night David had a chance to talk to Joe. As a loner, he had never felt adequate or comfortable in conversations like the one he needed to have with him. It was especially difficult seeing Joe so totally overcome with emotions of disbelief, anguish, grief, bitterness, anger and even loneliness.

He tried to begin by saying, "Joe, I am so sorry about Josena. It was a complete shock. I know there is a burning hole in your heart right now. I know it will never heal and go away completely, but I think in time it will get better."

Joe didn't look up or respond.

David had seen so many he loved die.

His thoughts formed more clearly and, full of rare passionate emotion, he continued, "Joe, hear me now. The feeling of love lives, but maybe it's like the ocean, full of conflict, full of pain. Sometimes it's for holding on and sometimes you must let go. Your love will never be lost. Your memories of love will always be of her. Let go now Joe. You must live."

Inexplicably, David's poetic soul had emerged to help his friend, but rarely, if ever, was it a help to himself.

Eleven

Joe looked up at him, his face so full of pain, and said, "Thank you David. I will let go but never forget. I just hate men like Taylor and Manford for the power they have over us and what they can get away with."

David agreed and said, "I understand. I have always hated men like that too, and for the same reason."

But David had dealt with trouble before. The next morning Josiah and David rode out of the barn on two horses.

Manford saw them and shouted, "Hey, where are you going?" David shouted back "North."

Seeing them getting away with the horses, Manford picked up his shotgun he always kept nearby. He fired both barrels over their heads. David drew his Colt revolver and shot Manford. The 44 caliber bullet struck him in the abdomen.

Joe shouted, "That gut shot should take about two hours to kill you."

Penelope's betrayal had been avenged, but her life could not be restored. It was an unchangeable finality.

They rode north toward Tennessee. Neither of them would see the Deep South again.

Twelve - Heading North

They rode their horses hard like two men in a hurry and on a mission. But they had nowhere to go and their purpose was to put the Deep South farther behind them. As fatigue set in, they stood up on their stirrups, holding onto the pommels, to ease their saddle soreness. They rested their horses in small towns where they could get them feed, water and livery. Up along the Tennessee River, they came to Shiloh.

Tennessee was a slave state but was pro-Union before the war. It was the last state to join the Confederacy. During the early part of the war, Grant had moved into southwestern Tennessee along the Tennessee River and fought at the battle of Shiloh, or the battle of Pittsburg Landing, on April 6-7, 1862. It was the beginning of his western campaign to gain control of the Mississippi River and valleys to the south. In the end, the Confederates were forced to retreat and Grant was victorious. But like many of his victories, casualties were very high.

The cities and capital in the east had no idea of the magnitude of the battle to come or the loss to follow. They were concentrating on the eastern theater in Virginia nearer by. The newspapers didn't report the scope of it beforehand or the extremity of it thereafter. There were virtually no photographers on hand to take pictures of the aftermath. But it was going to be a monumental confrontation with over 110,000 men engaged. The infantry was enhanced by an assembly of the greatest artillery heretofore.

With Grant's plan to gain control of the all-important Mississippi, cut the Confederacy in half and prohibit its use of the river to supply the South, he started north on the Tennessee. Two great armies formed there just north of the

Twelve

Tennessee - Kentucky border. The Confederates had two forts to protect the strategic area at the point where the Tennessee and the Cumberland pass close to each other flowing northward out of Tennessee. With the aid of Andrew Foote's Federal ironclad gunboats, Grant and his forces bombarded Fort Henry, won an easy victory and Confederate commander Lloyd Tilghman surrendered. Fort Donaldson was more difficult but was also defeated. Confederate General Albert Johnston had reinforced it; but Grant defeated him.

The next objective was Nashville. Johnston decided to abandon Nashville, retrench southward and hold the Confederate defense at Murfreesboro. Grant confronted him there and was successful.

With these Confederate defeats as precursors, the Federal and Confederate forces met together for the monumental battle at Pittsburg Landing near Shiloh Church. There the two armies resolved to face each other in full force.

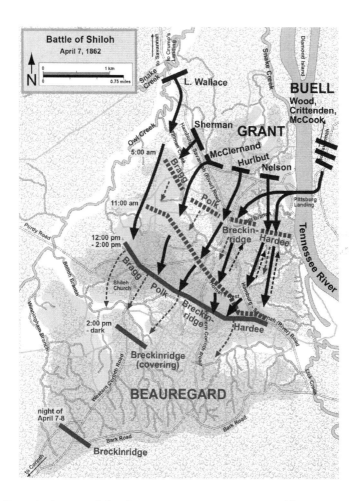

Grant's Army of the Tennessee was supported by Don Carlos Buell's Army of the Ohio, William T. Sherman and other generals.

William Tecumseh Sherman was born in 1820 in Ohio and was appointed to the West Point Military Academy as a 16-year-old in order to graduate in 1840. Ulysses S. Grant graduated from the Point just later in 1843. Sherman and

Grant became friends and Cump served under him in the Civil War. Together they brought the war to its conclusion with Grant's final efforts in Virginia and Sherman's in Tennessee, Georgia and South Carolina.

The Battle of Shiloh was Sherman's first major test under Grant. He was reckless and unprepared but managed to rally his division and conduct an orderly, fighting retreat that helped avert a disastrous Union rout.

Finding Grant at the end of the day sitting under an oak tree in the darkness and smoking a cigar, Sherman felt some wise and sudden instinct not to mention retreat.

In what would become one of the most notable conversations of the war, Sherman said simply: "Well, Grant, we've had the devil's own day, haven't we?"

After a puff of his cigar, Grant replied calmly: "Yes. Lick 'em tomorrow, though."

His performance was praised by Grant and Halleck and, after the battle, he was promoted to major general of volunteers, effective May 1, 1862.

They shared a common persecution from the newspaper reporters who referred to Grant as a drunk and Sherman as a lunatic. Sherman and Grant both had a longstanding addiction to cigar smoking. It is not known who smoked the most in a day but it is believed that they each smoked twenty of them. Grant maintained a trunk full of cigars in the tent of his many field command headquarters throughout the war.

Grant and Sherman shared a field headquarters at one point in the war and Grant saved Sherman embarrassment by meeting him out in the woods on horseback for informal military strategy meetings. Grant would sit on his horse and observe field movements from the high ground with Sherman's company. On those occasions they sat in the rain, Grant would become irritable when the cigars he kept in his pocket became soaked and couldn't be lit. Cump would have the presence of mind to remain silent.

At Shiloh, Grant met Johnston's Army of the Mississippi, who was replaced after his death by P.G.T. Beauregard. The Confederates were under-manned, ill-equipped but resolute. The confrontation was devastating. The carnage after two days was nearly 24,000 dead, wounded or missing. The Union killed and wounded were over 10,000. The Confederate killed or wounded were a little less. The captured or missing on both sides were nearly 4,000.

As for the accolades and blame and shame among the Union leaders, the debate raged. Who were the winners and who were the losers? Who could claim victory and who made critical errors? This would be a problem that would eventually be resolved later in the war. Grant would prevail and emerge as the leader and winner despite his antagonists.

But as the battle of Pittsburgh Landing approached, Grant was plagued with the idea that his superior, General Henry Halleck, was always scrutinizing him, hated him, and would find a way to destroy his career. He hoped there would come a time when Halleck would stretch the belief in his own magnificence too far. Maybe Lincoln would see that Halleck led armies from behind his desk in his headquarters and decide to demote him.

This was the last war where men would line up in wide columns, face each other across an open field, and mow each other down in volleys. They would fall in alternating waves as each side reloaded their muzzle loaded rifles after expending them with a single shot at the other side. This was the old Napoleonic traditional way taught at the Point. But with modern repeating weapons, this was foolhardy and certain death with no honor. Their rifled barrels were more accurate than the smooth bore muskets no longer used since the Mexican War. Lee would listen to Longstreet and be the first to begin to use fortification and trench defensive warfare.

***

Joe and David met some local people in town while stabling their horses. A man told them that the battle had been the bloodiest of any up to its time. For Joe, the sight of the abandoned fields and graves was surreal. It was foreign to his experience since he had been isolated at Savannah Oaks during the war.

For David, all the memories of his battles came flooding back - Antietam in Maryland, Battle of the Wilderness in Virginia and others.

He thought, 'So many young men had risen, dressed and eaten that morning. They had run bravely into battle and then they were gone. Every moment of their lives was reduced to that single misfortune. Only the dead have seen the end of war.' His mind was overwhelmed, his heart sickened.

Twelve

As silent unnoticed tears streamed down David's face, Joe began to gain a deeper understanding for what the horrors of the war had meant to his friend. David was quiet and withdrawn.

David looked up at Joe and said, "My God, this was happening three years ago here in April of the same year I was fighting back east at Antietam in September. We were killing each other everywhere."

Joe wanted to help but wasn't sure how. David kept everything inside. He wondered whether, just as David had helped him deal with the knowledge of Josie's death, he would be able to help David deal with his pain and suffering. But it wasn't in his nature to share his feelings. David had always relied on his journal as an outlet for his deep and sometimes dark troubled thoughts.

Just as he had done for him, Josiah reached out a hand to his friend's shoulder to offer comfort. Suddenly for David, it was as if the dam inside him broke. He found himself sharing with Josiah all the memories that were flooding his mind as he stood there.

He remembered Antietam in '62 and the long lines of the blue and the gray. He watched as so many fell and so many died. He saw the men thrown into the air and their bodies blown apart by the artillery. There was so much blood and so many bodies. At first they fell by the dozens. Finally they lay by the hundreds and the thousands. There was nothing noble or romantic about war for the men there.

He remembered hearing some of Lincoln's words spoken at Gettysburg, ".... that from these honored dead we take increased devotion to that cause for which they gave the last full measure of devotion - that we here resolve that these dead shall not have died in vain - that this nation, under God, shall have a new birth of freedom .... ."

When he finished talking, he wept silently for several minutes and then stared without expression across the field. He would never forget. The war was over, but the memories were fresh and raw. For the country, those memories were bitter and would last for generations.

While he had always understood to a degree the losses of those who had fought for his freedom, Joe now saw it closer and more personal. He understood that David and they had fought for his freedom. He would always respect and love him and them for that.

David understood that, at its deepest core, what it means to be human is the will to survive. A man's true character is his willingness to live. Without that, he will lay down and die.

He looked over at Joe, and thought about him. He thought about what Joe had been through, what he had suffered, and what he had lost. He thought about Joe's life in bondage and his loss of Josie. Yet Joe wanted to go on. He wanted to survive. He wanted to live.

"Do you want to stay here for a while David?"

"Just for this afternoon and tonight. Tomorrow we can head out."

With no plan in mind, they followed the Tennessee River north to Kentucky. They had been traveling since early morning. Yesterday had been a gut-wrenching, emotional trial for both of them.

In the lush farmland up along the Tennessee, they came to a secluded meadow grown up with alfalfa. Joe looked over at David and saw that his friend looked more worn and haggard than usual.

He called out, "Let's stop for a while and rest the horses."

"Sounds like a good idea Joe. They can graze for a while."

They dismounted and walked their horses by the reins toward the field.

"Let's take the saddles off so they can relax", David suggested.

There was a stand of willow trees along a stream back away from the road toward the field. They let the horses loose and filled their canteens with the cool water. They sat down, leaned against a willow and watched the horses drinking and splashing in the water - David's old dun mare, Joe's young bay roan cavorting in this peaceful place. As they sat there resting, with the sound of the stream gurgling in the background, a measure of peace settled on both of them from the respite and this place.

Joe said, "They got the right idea and that alfalfa will be good feed for them. They have earned it."

The horses came out of the stream and romped in the field while they ate their fill. The two friends rested quietly under the trees, lost in their own thoughts. After a while Joe took some hardtack out of his gunnysack and gave David a stick to gnaw on.

David noticed that Joe seemed to be a little sadder than usual. He asked him softly, "How are you feeling Joe?"

"I don't know for sure. Feels like it was me that was gut shot, not Manford."

"If you are feelin' guilty about him, you don't need to. He had it comin' when he shot at us with his shotgun", David replied.

"I guess so, but we can't blame him for all the troubles."

"You forgive too easy Joe."

Joe thought about it for a minute and explained, "I got to if I want to live with myself. The Lord gives me the strength and shows me what's best to do."

"Wish I had your faith. I cannot accept the authority or injustice of another. That gets in the way. That is just how I am. But life just keeps disappointing."

"How are you feeling about the war now, David?"

"I can't get all the pictures out of my head, especially after we saw the aftermath at Shiloh. It keeps comin' back, especially when I try to sleep. I try to write about it in my journal. That helps a little. Mostly I feel guilty since I survived and they didn't."

Twelve

There didn't seem to be much more of anything to say, so both men just sat there with their private thoughts.

David wondered, 'Is faith in myself enough? Can I manage my burden alone? There are things beyond my understanding.'

Josiah thought, 'He can't see God as a help, only another authority he has to fight.'

"David, God loves us. If we can feel, we can love. If we can love, we can believe. He gets us started. Puts the Spirit there. At the end, He will bring us home."

David looked at him and smiled, remained silent.

Twelve

Thirteen - Journey's End

They moved on and followed the Ohio River east. They traveled for a few days and both of them chose not to bring up talk of the war again. It was too painful for them and the wounds were still raw. They rode along and took a lighter road of conversation as David told Joe the exciting tales of his adventures at sea as a young man. He hoped that this would bring a smile to Joe's face and keep both their minds off all the painful memories.

They arrived in Covington late one afternoon. Joe spotted a boardinghouse and suggested they check in to bed down for the night. As they rode into town, the people in town looked at them askance. This wasn't the first time they had encountered this reaction. Two different looking men traveling together was not a usual sight, even in this area. But no one caused any trouble.

Joe and David were pleased to slow down and rest for a while. They stayed for two days to reconnoiter and regroup. The people became more friendly once they got to talk to them and know them a bit.

Joe and David were relaxing on the porch and looking at the lights of the big city across the Ohio. The reflections on the water were peaceful and somehow reassuring.

David said, "That's Cincinnati Joe."

"It looks exciting", he responded.

"Tomorrow we can go over and look around. It will be your first big city in the north. This will be as new an experience for you as my first visit to big cities in the South. I sure hope you like it."

Joe smiled, said "I think I will like it and look forward to it."

They sat quietly for a long time on the porch, with their feet on the railing, and watched the peaceful scene across the river. David was thinking about Joe's life and his own.

He looked at Joe's contented expression and said, "You know, a free man has to learn what it means to be himself. I'm still trying to figure that out myself."

Joe smiled at him and said, "It's all new to me, but I know what you mean. It's a great blessing to be able to do that and find out what it means for each of us as individuals. We will figure it out. What's best for each of us."

Troubled with guilt for holding back so long, David decided it was time to reveal the secret he had been keeping.

With a serious expression he said, "Joe, there's something I have to tell you. I couldn't do it until now because I didn't think you could bear any more. Back at Drish plantation, Manford told me that Josie had had a girl child a while after she arrived there."

Joe looked at him in shocked disbelief, cried out and sobbed, "Why didn't you tell me? That was my daughter. Where is she? We must find her."

David carefully replied, "He said they sold her off to a man in Mobile. I'm afraid she is long gone by now. We'll never find her Joe."

He waited quietly by his side. He knew there were no more words could be said to bring comfort. All he could do was be there as Josiah had been for him when friendship was most needed.

With a clarity of understanding and resignation Joe said, "Yeah, it's too late now for me to find her. But how can I forget her? I can never forget her. As much as my heart aches, I must find comfort in knowing that I have a daughter who was the result of my love for Josie. I can only pray that she will have the kind giving heart of her mother, and that God blesses her life."

"She will Joe, God knows she will."

The next morning they rode over the brand new suspension bridge and saw the cityscape of the city called the "Paris of America". The population was over 160,000 at the time, making it one of the largest cities in the country. The two men hitched their horses and took in the sights of the bustling city on foot. They saw the Music Hall, the Cincinnatian Hotel and the Shillito Department Store. They saw the Miami and Erie Canal completed in 1841 that originated from the Great Miami River.

Cincinnati had been the headquarters for the Department of the Ohio and a major source of supplies and troops for the Union during the war. However, it did participate in commerce with slave states and did have many southern sympathizers.

———————————◦○◦———————————

While they enjoyed their stay there, the city life had no lasting appeal for either of them. They made their way 50 miles north to the small hamlet of Hamilton. This place looked right to them - lots of space, beautiful land, and some friendly people.

After they arrived in Hamilton, they sought their opportunities and laid the groundwork to develop their own individual, separate lives. Together they sold their labor once again and pooled their savings. With this stake, Joe bought a small farm outside town. David kept his horse in the barn there with Joe's. His dun mare died later that summer. They buried her on the back of Joe's property.

David got a place in town where he could keep a small apartment over his carpentry shop. They remained close friends and shared Sunday dinners every week at Joe's farm.

The general hardware store in Hamilton tried to carry everything the community needed. The owner would special order anything not on hand to better serve them. Joe frequented there often to purchase all his basic woodworking tools. He accumulated saws, block planes, chisels, wood scrapers, awls and drills. In a brief time, he outfitted a partition of his barn and established the Ashford Furniture Company.

After he opened his furniture business, his reputation quickly grew and his shop was always busy. His furniture was in great demand by the more affluent whites, freeborn blacks and newly prosperous freedman. He became known throughout the region for the unique artisanship, quality and durability of his products. His graceful chairs, tables and break-fronts became sought after. The unique carvings and finishes of Ashford pieces became his signature and hallmark.

His personal reputation grew with both black and white people in the area. He was held in high regard by everyone for his intelligence and optimistic forward-looking view. With his name and reputation for integrity so well known throughout his region, he was elected as the honorable congressman Josiah Ashford representing his local district for the Ohio state government. As a male property owner, he had legal qualification to vote and hold office. His life was busy and full with his growing business and his many newfound friendships.

He lovingly remembered Josena but was happy with his emergence from bondage and the direction of his life's trajectory. David remained his steadfast supporter and brother in the cause for justice.

Joe continued his lifelong learning process. He read less literature now, but read extensively in law, philosophy, economics and political science. He read Adam Smith, Lincoln, Frederick Douglass, de Tocqueville, Milton, Shakespeare and the Bible. He expressed his intellect externally - became a gifted orator crowds gathered to hear. His friend David expressed his intellect differently - internally with his private writing of poetry and observations of the human condition.

Joe attended the Baptist Church in Hamilton and became a member and an elder. He was a role model and leader for the freedmen. The congregation was mostly black freedmen, but included some freeborn Negroes and a few whites who felt no discomfort with the people and their worship. David often attended and enjoyed the working class people he had always gravitated toward.

By 1877, most of the post-war Reconstruction efforts had ceased in the South and state governments there had swept away most of the progress made by the 13th, 14th, and 15th amendments to the Constitution. In the North, steady progress was being made for social justice. The Republican party of Abraham Lincoln had continued to hold the Presidency throughout the post-war years of Reconstruction. Andrew Johnson, Ulysses Grant and Rutherford Hayes from Ohio each brought their personality to a moderate reform movement that met with some success in the North.

In his region, Joe was greatly admired by freeborn Negroes as a former slave and first generation freedman who displayed exceptional grit, achievement and character. In his case, they were able to set aside their view of superiority as freeborn Negroes. His fellow freedmen looked up to him as their leader and kinsman. Many whites put aside bigotry and saw him for the exceptional man that he was. He was well liked throughout southwestern Ohio and well accepted as their reliable man of dependable character to represent them in the Ohio state government.

Time passed. His bay roan had died and he buried him alongside David's. He bought a new, high-spirited young filly more suitable for a carriage than a saddle. Joe traveled to Columbus whenever the legislature was in session. On one return trip, he stopped in the hardware store to check the shelves to see if the dowel stock he had asked for had come in. He was still wearing his tweed suit, vest and tie from his trip.

His friend Roy was running the store and greeted him, "Hi Joe. How did the session go?"

Joe smiled and replied, "We're still talking about land sub-division requirements. I hope we get it settled soon."

Roy nodded and said, "Me too. A lotta newcomers are moving in and want to start small farms."

It was true. More Germans and Scots-Irish were coming from the east. Freedmen were coming from the South. They were all looking for their portion of the old, agrarian Jeffersonian American dream. The large landholders were selling off their vast holdings to new people trying to settle their lives and raise their families.

While they were discussing politics and conducting their business, an elegant young black woman came into the store looking for some cloth material to make new curtains. She was well dressed, prim and proper, and a refined lady.

She asked, "Roy, any new material come in this week?"

Roy said, "No, not yet. Mary, let me introduce you to Congressman Ashford. Joe, this is Mary Custis."

"Pleasure meeting you ma'am. Roy didn't mention my real job. I make custom furniture for the folks in the area."

"Do you mean Ashford furniture? Everybody has heard of that. Forgive me if I sound forward, but you must come visit my family. My father and mother would be honored to meet you as our congressman and good neighbor."

"Always a pleasure to meet the constituents, Mary. Sometimes new furniture customers too. Ha ha."

Mary Custis was the 3rd generation of freeborn Negroes descending from Martha Custis Washington's dowry slaves from Mount Vernon, Virginia. Unlike the freeman or freedman, their generations had never worn a slave collar. Her family had lived in Hamilton for years and was prominent and respected in the community.

Thirteen

This auspicious meeting in May 1868 between her and Josiah would change the direction of their lives.

Fourteen - Home

Mary and Josiah began a friendship which developed into a deep relationship. For Josiah, it was not the youthful passionate love he had felt for Josena during their bondage, but a free deeper lasting, mature love. She found Josiah to be a dear companion. They both shared fine minds with common interests in literature and philosophy. Mary had almost given up hope of finding a man like him.

In Mary, Josiah found a warm loving woman, not a young girl, but someone who was worldly, intelligent, with a humorous and witty nature that made life a joy for him. She was everything he could have wanted if he had written out a description.

In a short time, they were viewed in the eyes of the community as the couple to watch. Their marriage was a community affair attended by Josiah's friends from the state legislature, the freeborn Negroes from Mary's circles, and black and white farmers and merchants and professionals from the area. With Mary's best girlhood white friend as Maid-of-Honor and David as Best Man, the bridal party made a striking group.

They were family coming together for devotion and community. For all they had been through together, David and Josiah felt a love as brothers who had come home.

By August, southwestern Ohio usually had oppressive heat and humidity like the Deep South. But on their late spring June wedding day, the weather was a blessing. The sun shone brightly, the air was dry and comfortable, and soft billowy clouds drifted slowly across the blue sky. Gentle breezes ruffled the fresh leaves, while the sweet smell of wisteria entered and permeated the church.

The church was filled to capacity with friends and community. As the wedding march sounded on the organ, Mary came down the aisle on her father's arm. She wore a stylish white satin gown with a flowing train. Joe wore his finest white linen suit with black suspenders and black cravat, topped off by his best Sunday straw hat.

With David at his side, Josiah watched her come down the aisle. For a fleeting moment, he remembered that day long past when he and Josena had jumped over the broom and had their humble African marriage ceremony. But when he saw the smile on Mary's face, the memory quickly faded and he smiled back with moist eyes as he returned to the complete happiness of the present. As they joined hands to take their vows, he felt that he was the luckiest man in the world to have been blessed, to have found love again, with such a wonderful woman.

The reception at the town square lasted all afternoon with dining, dancing and joyful wishes from everyone in attendance. Mary's parents were thrilled that she had found a good, sound, truly Christian man to share her life with.

They renovated Joe's old farmhouse and converted it into a beautiful large country home just outside the town. Their home became something like an annex for the Ohio state capital in Columbus for the citizens of the Hamilton region. There were many political meetings and rallies there with Joe officiating and Mary entertaining. David would share his historical perspectives and experiences to contribute to the deliberations.

With their marriage settled in and their love deepened and grown, they pleasantly surprised their friends and community, when a year after their wedding, Mary gave birth to twins, a boy they named David and a girl they named Josena.

With his factory located on the farm property, Josiah's home-based business and success afforded him the opportunity to spend time with his children and actively participate in rearing them. Later, in his old age when they had moved on in the world, he would count this among his greatest blessings.

As time passed and the children grew, they listened to conversations at the dinner table and watched the adult meetings in the parlor from the staircase across the foyer. The household was always alive with guests and animated discussions.

Mary explained to them what it meant to be freeborn, just as she was and they were. She told them about the Revolutionary War and George Washington, the first President, and how his wife Martha Custis Washington owned her own slaves as part of her dowry. When they were freed upon her death, some of the Custis line of former slaves had moved west out into the Northwest Territory and ended up here in Ohio.

When uncle David came to dinner, he told them about President Lincoln, the Civil War - the long four-year tragedy - required to preserve the Union and end slavery. They discussed the political events leading up to it and the southern argument of social Darwinism asserting the fundamental inferiority of Negroes to justify slavery.

David explained to them the distinction between slavery and racism, now that racism had increased with the parting of the slaveholders and the enslaved. Joe told his children what slavery had been like for him as a young man in Missouri under the task system, and later in Mississippi under the harsher gang system employed to grow short staple cotton. They both gave them the perspective of the clash of cultures and economics.

The children were eager and attentive students. They understood the sadness, loss and sacrifice that had been made to rid America of the sin and shame of slavery. They understood the bitterness that remained, and would remain for many years to come.

The Ashford home was awash with the ideas of the human spirit and the ideals of the American experience. Their father explained to them the distinction between the balanced concepts of social justice and civil rights versus individual responsibility, community service and societal obligation. The children would grow up grounded in the important values. They understood that their extended family had directly participated in - been directly a part of - so much American history.

Joe's business grew and the old barn would not do. He needed to build a larger building dedicated to just the Ashford Furniture Company. David helped him and, together as before, they accomplished their job. This time they built a magnificent factory. They outfitted the building with large work tables and wood clamps and fixtures to hold glued joints. They built racks for organizing wood storage. David brought innovation to the manufacturing process. He invented, designed and built machinery to plane wood surfaces and remove the unnecessary manual work that didn't affect the craftsmanship of the finished product.

Joe formed alliances with his suppliers - the saw mills in the region. He visited them personally to select the best woods for his furniture. He eventually hired a staff of twelve workers to look after the many manual labor and management tasks to keep up with the growth. Appreciating how fortunate he had been to have learned a skill as a slave, he felt a responsibility to help freedmen who came to the area seeking a new life. He hired and trained as many as he could as his furniture business grew. He discovered that he enjoyed teaching others much in the same way Ben had worked with him. He delegated a lot of the work but kept a vigilant eye on the quality to assure that his artistry did not get lost.

Joe had found a lasting satisfaction and a complete happiness grounded in love and family. His family prospered. The area where they lived did too. He was home.

With Joe's influence, young David and Josena were permitted to attend classes at Miami University of Ohio in 1889. They were not permitted to graduate, and it wasn't until 1906 that Nellie Craig graduated there as the first African-American.

Joe asked his daughter, "How are your studies at college coming along?"

Josie looked worried and wasn't sure how to say it but said, "Papa, Dave and I are doin' fine in our studies, but those white folks are only gonna let us take a few courses because you are the big congressman. They ain't gonna let us finish and graduate."

Joe, looking upset said, "Is that right honey? First of all, you need to learn how to speak properly if you expect to get ahead in this world. You meant to say 'Dave and I are doing fine' and 'the college administration won't let us finish and graduate.' Second, you should have come to me with this sooner. We'll look for another way to do this. There are other colleges. Go find Dave. We need to talk about this."

"OK Papa, I'll go get him. We talked to uncle David about this and he got angry at the university. He said we must come and tell you about it."

They held a family meeting to discuss college plans for the twins. Joe and Mary tried to give the young ones a fair ear, but made sure that they provided parental guidance to their young, immature, and sometimes impetuous, dear children. Uncle David was invited to give his perspective. They knew he cared deeply for the welfare of their children.

Joe offered his best idea for them. He told them about the new Oberlin College - founded in 1833 - up near Cleveland. It was a school with strong programs in music and theology, and with emphasis on all the humanities - English literature, the Roman and Greek classics, philosophy, sociology, anthropology, religion, history, government and political science. There, blacks and whites studied together, grounded in the classics and humanities, with unique opportunities available to study the ideas and writings of great leaders like Frederick Douglass and Abraham Lincoln, and to learn about social justice and new directions for civil rights.

Young Josie and Dave became encouraged and grew excited about this solution. It seemed to be the very best for them and their parents' wishes. They decided to transfer to Oberlin and set a course for a brighter new direction for their young lives.

———————○C———————

From the earliest colonial days, even while the Revolutionary War was being fought, and long before mercantilism would be usurped by industrialization, the early American pioneers and settlers were pushing westward to establish their lives for themselves and their families. Thomas Jefferson recognized this and had a vision for an agrarian society of small independent farmers and landowners as property owners - the Jeffersonian yeoman freeholders - as the basis for the American dream.

In those days, Ohio was the western frontier and the earliest remote inland region to establish farms and a rural American society. The founders and framers of the Constitution wrote the Northwest Ordinance of 1787 as a model to define how all new territories would be established. As one of the founding documents, it defined the conditions under which territories would be sub-divided to become future states.

It was about the land - how it should be allocated, divided and owned - and how society should be governed. It determined that slavery would be prohibited in this and all future territories. It allotted land for educational use so that schools would be built. It required freedom of religious practice for its citizens. For the future of America's development, it was an all-important document.

In Josiah's time, the Ohio legislature would convene in early summer - between planting and harvesting - to deliberate matters of governance and law for the citizens of Ohio. Land use, and related matters, was still a political issue to be deliberated and resolved for them, their futures and their livelihood.

He drove to Columbus in his carriage for the main session each June. On some occasions he brought Mary and the children with him as a family trip and for the education of his son and daughter. His family was permitted to view the floor of the session from the visitors' gallery.

The speaker rapped his gavel and announced, "Order, order. Gentlemen, this session is hereby convened. We are called here today in our assembly to deliberate, decide and vote on Ohio senate bill SR403 passed by our esteemed colleagues in the Ohio senate. I call before you our esteemed colleague from the southwestern region, the Honorable Josiah Ashford, to present its matters before you."

The leader looked to his right at Josiah and raised his hand upward in his direction, "Congressman Ashford."

Josiah rose from his seat, walked to the podium and shook the speaker's hand. He looked out at the assembly, paused to look across the room and smiled. He stood bolt upright and with his left thumb in his suspenders and right hand raised in the air, spoke to his colleagues.

His face turned to its characteristic resolve as he spoke eloquently and clearly:
"Speaker, esteemed colleagues, we find ourselves at a crucial moment. What we decide today will affect our constituents - our people, our citizens, our families - for the remainder of their lives and for the lives of their descendents to follow.

The great Ordinance of 1787 gave us a plan and guidance to follow. It provided land for schools. The schools were built. But education has been left to us - the great state of Ohio to resolve for ourselves. Much has changed since then; much has run afoul. I will speak to you about that today. We have the opportunity, the authority and the responsibility to change that, correct that and rectify that."

The room was silent in rapt attention. He continued:
"The intent of our founders was clear. We would establish a great nation to the extent of its boundaries, not even known at that time, where free men would live their lives and prosper under the grace of God, as no nation had ever done before."

Loud cheers and applause broke out and drowned Josiah's words. The speaker rapped his gavel for several moments and spoke out, "Attention! Attention! Call to order!"

The room returned to silence and Josiah continued to speak: "Many of our aspirations have come to pass to fulfill our original ideals. We have turned around the subversions of our southern fellow citizens with the sacrifice of the blood and treasure of our people. Abraham Lincoln brought us to that eventuality and shall ever be remembered for the salvation and redemption of our nation."

The room remained silent in anticipation. He continued:
"Today we have many laws establishing the rights of property owners and for our citizens to vote and hold public office. Our schools are flourishing, our children are benefitting from this, and our country is improving."

They waited for his next words:

"But there is more to be done. There is always more to be done. We will never achieve perfection, but we must strive for it, reach up for it, as Americans and God loving human beings.

We have before us SR403. It will guarantee equal access to higher education for all our children without regard to the color of their skin. It will be based on the content of their character and our character. Surely, honor and integrity will compel us to pass this as the right thing to do. I urge you to vote for it in the affirmative."

Applause broke out one last time as Josiah returned to his seat. Assembly bill SR403 was passed by a narrow margin. It ratified and finalized the senate bill that preceded it. Citizens of all races would attend Ohio's educational institutions. Mary and the children understood that Josiah had played an important part in this change. They were proud of him.

———————◦◦◦———————

David benefited from the expansion of small farms in the Hamilton area also. The agriculture in Ohio was primarily based on wheat. This area, and the Midwest in general, was the "Old Wheat Belt". Other cash and subsistence crops were grown also - corn, rye, buckwheat, oats, barley, potatoes, meadow (feed grasses for animals), clover, sorghum, tobacco. The Miami Valley area especially grew tobacco as a precious cash crop.

The balance of subsistence and cash crops farming on small plots proved smarter than the agriculture in the South for its time. Huge agri-business corporations would come later and farther in the west.

Fourteen

David renovated the older farm buildings, built new houses and barns, and soon became the man to go to for the newcomers to the area. He studied architectural and mechanical engineering books and learned more about structures. He became a designer and self-educated architect. When the time was appropriate, he hired two workers to take over the heavy lifting and mundane tasks. He prospered too.

One gray Monday morning, David was in town to go to the hardware store for some supplies. He had stayed over at the farm after Sunday dinner with Joe, Mary and the young ones. He came into the store and saw Roy at the counter.

"Good mornin' Roy. Looks like some rain comin' later today."

"I expect so David. What brings you in today?"

"I need a keg of ten-penny nails if you got them."

"Yep. I do. Just a minute. I'll bring them in from out back."

David noticed two men outside on the street talking. He hadn't seen them before.

"Here you go David. That'll be $1.50."

"Thanks. Oh, I'll need a small, flat bastard file to sharpen my saw teeth too."

"That's another 50 cents."

David put the file in his pocket and hoisted up the heavy keg, hugging it to his chest. Roy said his goodbye and watched

David go out the front door, still with his slight limp. David lifted the keg of nails into the back of his wagon. He looked over at the two men, thought they were farmers.

He walked over and said, "Good morning. Haven't seen you fellows before. I'm David Wexley."

The bigger man with the beard said, "Hello. I'm Jeremiah Johnston and this is Bill Wallis."

"Are you settling here and starting a farm?"

The smaller man said, "Oh no. We are from Buffalo, New York and just passing through, heading west."

David saw they were drifters like he had been much of his life.

He learned they were Union veterans and had fought in Virginia and the Carolinas. They sat down on the sidewalk bench and told each other their war stories. They learned that the three of them had fought at Antietam that day.

Bill told him, "Jeremiah and I fought with the 4th New York Volunteers, 3rd Brigade, 3rd Division, 2nd Corps under Lieutenant Colonel John McGregor. We lost a lot of our boys that day at the Sunken Road when A. P. Hill drove us back."

David said, "We did too. I lost a good friend, Geoff Braxton when we charged over the Burnside Bridge. I had worked with him as a carpenter apprentice in Baltimore before the war. We signed up together and fought under General Burnside's command. I knew him a long time and we saw a lot together. It was brutal how fast we took casualties."

He surprised himself that he could talk about it so dispassionately now.

He was curious about what they intended to do now and asked, "What's your plan for out west, Bill?"

"We don't know for sure, but there is a lot going on out there and lots of opportunities since they finished the railroad in '69."

Jeremiah said, "They started the Pacific railroad in '63 while we were all still fighting the war. Now you can link up to it in Iowa and go all the way to California."

It was true. The new transcontinental railroad was built to connect the end of the eastern railroad in Council Bluffs, Iowa and Omaha, Nebraska on the Missouri River to Sacramento, California. The project began at each end by two working crews and met at Promontory Summit in Utah to drive in the last spike, uniting the two halves, the Union Pacific Railroad and the Central Pacific Railroad, together. A railroad bridge was completed across the Missouri to finalize the connection in 1873.

David asked Jeremiah again, "Where are you planning to go and what will you do out there?"

He answered, "We might go to Colorado and work construction or mining. If that doesn't pan out, we'll head farther west and see what opportunities there are on the Pacific coast in California or Oregon."

David said, "Well it was good to meet you fellas and I wish you best of luck with your adventure."

Fourteen

This encounter with Jeremiah and Bill was intriguing to David. He missed the days when he had wandered and explored the country. He enjoyed meeting regular people and hearing about their experiences. But he was settled in Ohio and his life was peaceful. There was a freedom in this life too. Even with this newfound peace and freedom, his thoughts often drifted back to the troubled past.

Journal entry, October 12, 1879-

We were told, and we all believed, the war was just a rebellion and we would lick them and end it in a month or two. None of us knew how long it would last or the price we would pay. My view of slaveholders has not changed, nor will it ever do so. It is a good thing that the sin of slavery has been wiped away from our country forever. But I have learned, as I have always believed, that the poor whites in the South fought us as an invading force intent on burning down their farms and killing them. I can never blame them for fighting for their survival. It is a shame that they are forgotten in all the passions and death of those horrible times.

But finally, at last I have learned something of love – what it means to know and understand another human being and a tolerance for many, to care and put the other above you, beyond you, in place of you. This is God's grace and his plan.

Fourteen

He gained the respect of the community and formed many friendships with working-class people - black and white - with whom he had always felt a kinship. But he never had the good fortune to have a family.

Fourteen

Fifteen - Love Lost

During the late 19th century in Hamilton, Ohio, race relations were tentative but tolerable. There were no laws explicitly requiring segregation, but the community of small family farms formed a natural separation of the races. They kept to themselves and the area was generally peaceful. The races didn't mix and miscegenation was considered a deeper sin than incest. As a carryover from the abuses of slaveholders toward their black female property in the past, black people didn't take kindly to interracial marriage or sexual relations. Whites looked down on it as well based on their prejudices. It happened occasionally, but rarely, and was severely discouraged as a taboo by both races.

In town, blacks and whites traded in the same stores and ate at the same taverns, but worshipped in their separate churches. With some exceptions, parents naturally aligned their children in racially divided schools.

David worked and moved freely throughout both communities. He and his small crew built barns, farm houses and out-buildings for black families and white families. His foundation and framing carpenter John was white. His finish carpenter Sam was black. He was well liked and accepted by all his customers. They understood his views of tolerance and deep friendship with Josiah.

He and his men - John and Sam - were often invited to share a meal with the families he served on their farms. It was traditional for farm people to take their mid-day meal as the main meal for the day and as a long break from their work.

Fifteen

David met Estelle. The Culpeppers were a kindly and outgoing family and enjoyed the company and friendship of David when they contracted him repeatedly to help them expand their prosperous farm. Jim and Lucy Culpepper had three grown children - a daughter and two sons. Estelle was the oldest and well along toward spinsterhood. She was a beautiful and serene black woman with a quiet grace that attracted all that knew her.

Estelle and David felt a mutual attraction. She often watched him directing and working with his men as they erected new buildings. She saw the goodness in David and his strong spirit of justice in the treatment of people. She knew about his reputation and how much he was respected in the area.

She brought David and his men a pail of cool water on hot afternoons. It was a good reason to see him and they both looked forward to spending a few moments together. After their refreshment, she often stayed a while longer, hoping he might glance over her way and give her a smile.

David and Estelle talked about the crops and the weather and eventually the deeper things. They talked about the human things - kindness, forgiveness, acceptance and love. And they spoke of the spiritual things like God's grace and forbearance. They shared an intellectual view of life with the human heart as its source. They had not found this in the others in their lives. They fell in love.

He told her about his childhood in Baltimore and his time as a sailor. He told her about the horrors of the war and the friends he had lost. He told her about meeting Josiah, their long journey together and their long friendship.

Fifteen

She told him about her family and how grateful she was to be freeborn and raised in the North. Life had been good for her growing up in Hamilton. Sometimes though, it was lonely on the farm. They both had been lonely.

He took time from work and they walked across the fields into the meadows and to the forest at the end of the Culpepper property. Sometimes they met in their secret meadow away from all people, alone together in their enchanted place and time. Their lovemaking was gentle and giving with care for the other. Estelle caressed David's disfigured leg and looked through his eyes into his heart.

But this happiness was not to last. When Jim Culpepper learned of their relationship, he was upset. He ordered David to leave his property; to just gather his tools and his men and to go away immediately and never come back. This time David chose to not fight, but to comply. He believed it was best for Estelle and everyone else to obey her father's wishes.

With resignation, he stood in the pouring rain outside the barn and watched Estelle standing across the barnyard. The downpour soaked them both and it was difficult to see each other's faces. The rain made invisible the tears on David's face.

He stared at her across the yard with a pained smile and said, "I love you."

From that distance she could not hear his voice but understood the words and the expression on his face.

She answered back, "I love you", and David understood.

The love affair had caused no commotion in the community and David continued his work as before. He knew Estelle was a once-in-a-lifetime woman and would always be the irreplaceable love of his life. His bright hope had been dashed and he grew despondent.

———————————◦———————————

Whenever Josiah was not around to look after him, David spent his free time in the tavern. Whiskey became his solace and helped him to sleep at night. He drank too much. Too many nights he staggered back to his bed from the tavern. His men tried to talk to him and change his new destructive behavior.

Josiah knew what had happened and tried to bring David around. He was troubled that his best friend was falling in a downward spiral and might not survive it. He brought David to church with his family and hoped David would re-connect with them and take interest in young Josie and David as he had in the past.

David spent his evenings in the tavern and spent time with Jeremiah Johnston and Bill Wallis he had met on the street some weeks before. They had both come from Buffalo and continued to stay in Hamilton for a time. It reminded David of his nights in Baltimore before the war - before the age of innocence had ended. But like a firefly escaping his grasp, innocence had long ago escaped and could never be caught again.

Jeremiah and Bill told David they still planned to head west and would be leaving soon. They had decided by now they would split up, go in different directions and pursue different opportunities. Jeremiah told him he would head for Texas. Bill would go to Colorado. They promised to write David and keep him informed of their experiences and fortunes.

Jeremiah found east Texas an extension of the old Deep South but with promising differences. Cotton production was booming under large agriculture corporations with free labor. Galveston was growing as a new port to the Gulf of Mexico. The state was expansive and optimistic. A feeling of freedom was prevalent in this post-war economic boom. Opportunities were bountiful, with unanticipated new ones to come, for adventurous men of all ages and skills moving into the area.

Bill found the silver mining in Colorado to be a frantic rush, almost a panic, to find riches. Men were pouring into the area at a phenomenal rate as land was staked out and new mines were beginning every week. Towns were sprouting up from nowhere and people were moving in to service the boom. Bars, brothels, banks, assayers, livery and heavy machine equipment suppliers all benefitted from the insanity. Often they were the best winners. Law and order would come later. For now, it was a dangerous and wide-open place. Men had to have the skills to handle trouble on their own as it surely would come.

The Comstock Lode was discovered in 1859 and news of its discovery had set off the whole mad rush fueled by the insane thirst for quick riches. San Francisco had accumulated great wealth from the enterprise and California was growing faster than any area in America. Later in 1879, silver had been discovered in Colorado. It was exciting to work there in any capacity.

David heard from Jeremiah and Bill and thought, 'I wonder about Colorado. Maybe it's time for a fresh start.' He considered it for several weeks and became obsessed thinking about it and weighing it against his settled life in Ohio. He had so many friends here and knew what to expect for the future. But his life was static and maybe at a dead end. It would be painful to live here near Estelle and not be with her.

Finally he decided to talk to Josiah.

Joe told him, "David, it's not practical or a wise move for you, especially at your age. You have a good life here with many friends and people who care about you."

David thought and said, "I know it Joe. But I'm living on the sidelines here. You have fulfilled all your dreams and, with your life's work, you now are enjoying it's fruits. I cannot live my life as just a spectator watching you and Mary and young Josie and David from the sidelines. It isn't enough."

<hr />

He sold off his tools and equipment to John and Sam, said his goodbyes to everyone who mattered and, with his savings, took the railroad to Colorado. He went to work in mine safety construction. After a year, he had established himself as an engineer and architect with a crew working for him.

Mining for silver required blasting and digging to the fault line where the rich vein of the valuable mineral resided. The underground mines needed heavy support structure to maintain the access and safety of the tunnels to the working face deep within them. David and his crew built these heavy wooden beam supports. The work was lucrative and kept them busy.

There was no danger of fire in silver mining from explosive gases like the methane deposits so lethal in coal mining. But in

1900, there was a crisis at the mine David was servicing. A charge had been set off at the working face and the fault line shifted. The workers waiting outside heard the deep rumble after the planned explosion. The ground shook and a thick plume of gray stone dust poured out of the entrance.

After the movement had settled, David and his crew ran into the mine to check the shoring structure and make certain the roof had not collapsed. There was an aftershock at the face and the ceiling fell in behind them, trapping them inside. For three days crews dug through the rubble deeper into the mine until they found the crew. It was for naught. David and his crew had been killed instantly from the falling rock during the aftershock. Life is difficult and sometimes ends abruptly and unexpectedly.

As a matter of policy, all workers on the site had filed a Last Will and Testament with the mining company headquarters. Since he had no family, his had been very simple. It instructed that all his money and possessions would go to Josiah Ashford or his heirs in Hamilton, Ohio and that Josiah Ashford was to be executor to the will. He further requested that upon his death, subsequent to any local memorial service that might be given, his body was to be sent by railroad to Hamilton, Ohio and buried near the plots allocated for the Ashford family. Finally, he wished to have indentified on his grave marker or tombstone that he was a veteran of the Civil War and served with Baltimore's Light Guard Infantry.

The Wexley male line ended, and left no heirs, with the passing of Morgan and David. The Ashton male line continued from Josiah to David and to his children.

Fifteen

———————◦———————

Two ordinary men had borne great hardship and suffered extraordinary tragedy. Life was difficult, but both had survived. One had risen above it and managed to find home and happiness. One had not. Both had achieved a greatness; their lives mattered and made a difference to others.

Ultimately, they had lived their lives, and did what they did, as free men. And free men they were.

Epilogue

The one constant in life is that it brings changes. America was changing. After more than 20 years in one place, David had again grown restless and felt the pull of wanderlust. In 1887, when he was 55 years old, he needed to find things new - places, opportunities, life - once again. He had heard that men were mining silver in Colorado and that there were great opportunities in a place called Aspen. He needed to go West to see it for himself. This time he would go alone.

He had packed his old blanket roll and gunnysack. Joe went with him as far as Cincinnati. David took the railroad west to Colorado. He would remain in the West for the rest of his days.

On the day they parted, they clasped forearms in the old Roman way as men do that have great respect, admiration and affection for one another.

With his expression so typically formed with resolve, Joe had said, "I will never forget you. We have shared together so much of our lives. I will think of you always. God speed and be well my brother."

David smiled and with moist eyes, had said his last words to him, "You know me better than anyone in my life. You know I have to go. I will think about you and wish you were with me for all the new things I will discover and do. You are the best friend I have ever known and I will miss you the rest of my days."

David would remember the lessons of humanity he had learned from Josiah. He knew that for the human spirit to be human, it must be free. He died near Aspen the summer of 1900. His body was brought back to Hamilton and the Civil War

Society placed a fresh American flag next to his grave marker every year to honor his service.

Josiah knew that because of David, there was hope for free men to live in harmony. David had fought for his people but even more important, he had fought for him. He had kept the last poem David had written and sent him before his death. He read it at David's graveside memorial service.

Josiah died later in 1906 and was buried next to him in the Hamilton cemetery. At his funeral, David Ashford gave the eulogy and spoke of his father's life and the road he had helped pave for a better America - one that would someday realize its ideals. He told them how Josiah Ashford had chosen his given name - from a lifelong friend who supported him, defended him, loved him and helped him pave that road for justice. It was forty years ago.

The times of their lives were powerful and taught them life's most important lesson. David and Josiah learned that man is a sentient being above the beasts and below the angels. They learned from their individual lives and from each other that there are, and always will be, good men and bad men on the earth, but there is great value in good men finding each other and being together "by the better angels of our nature".

From David- For Josiah and others I have loved; I have made my peace-

I've known enough days now, I fear if I know more,

I'll become disenchanted with the ones I've known before.
So now in summertime, In summertime,
I'd like to go,

While there's still sun enough,
I want to go in summertime, in summertime, in summertime.

To die in silence, without a single sound,
To touch the earth as gently as a dead leaf,
when it hits the ground.

To leave behind a mem'ry soft as summertime,
For those one loves and has to leave behind.
To fold as softly as the grass blades fold,
When wild things trample them on mornings damp and cold.

To leave behind a fragrance, carried on the wind for those one loves and will never see again.

To die in summertime, or not die at all,
While I'm still running,
While I'm still running forward,
While I still own my own mind,
I want to go in summertime.

To Die in Summertime - Rod McKuen

_____ end _____

Acknowledgments

All of us are the product of our times and experiences. We see the history we live in and that our lives have phases. We learn and grow under the watchful eyes of our parents and learn the facts and ideas of the world from our teachers. We learn the skills to make a living and provide for ourselves on our own. We marry, raise our children and watch them grow, and learn, and go out, and forward the same as we.

I am grateful to my parents, teachers, and my loving wives. I am proud of my children and the lives they have made for themselves. After seven decades of life, I thought it was time to put down the mantle, relish my remaining time, and enjoy the fruits and blessings life has brought me.

Sometimes life can take unexpected turns, open unexpected doors, and bring new self-discovery. It can happen at any time and surprise us. I have always gravitated toward younger people as my friends and co-workers, especially more so as the decades have rolled on. There are two who have inspired and have come along at this twilight juncture. There are two more who have cared and helped, one who stands close by and one appearing from the distant past.

Thank you Abraham, my African son, for teaching me what it means to be human. Thank you for your lessons of courage, resilience of the human spirit, perseverance and faith.

Thank you Jim, my passionate teacher. You are my professor, but I call you teacher for its higher meaning. I have known a lot of the facts for many years, but you have opened my eyes to the meanings. You taught me to feel history. Thank you for awakening my passion for learning and igniting my love for history and writing. The ideas are planted now and need to grow, mature, and be harvested.

Thank you Nick, my literary and insightful son. You have been with me every step of the way; patiently reading it all, discussing it all, analyzing it all, and the sounding board for the important ideas.

Thank you Joan. As my old friend, so long far way, you have appeared back in my life when I needed you most. As a teacher of teachers, I couldn't have hoped for a better mentor, editor and partner. You believed. Your generous words were your gifts to me. I understand you now. Your words - words of writing, words of ideas, words of encouragement - were gifts of love and friendship. Your gifts made a poor book a good one. You brought me the last mile.

Author's Comments

Writing narrative is easy. It flows along like a river. Writing dialogue is more challenging. It requires knowing your characters intimately, how they think, and what they care about. The visuals of the settings and the story action attract the mind, but in the end, the characters capture the heart. It is more accurate to say that my characters revealed themselves to me, rather than that I created them. They often surprised me and I learned important things from them. For its writer, a book can be a catharsis, with teaching moments that test the truths and falsehoods of his beliefs. Hopefully, this will inform the reader in this same manner.

The storyline is centered around 1865. Some historical events were described with detail to build drama. Others were merely alluded to in passing since they would be familiar to readers. The story portrays the power of friendship in deeply troubled times. It is a blend of political, military and social histories and uses fictional characters to tell the story, with historical figures to provide the backdrop.

I visited Andersonville in 1987 and never forgot the sadness I felt there. The village and prison camp are an historic site. At present, the long rows of graves are arranged neatly and marked with aged alabaster stones spread across a beautiful green field for visitors to reflect upon. Many have names with dates of birth. The dates of their deaths were all within a year of each other.

The village and site are near Oglethorpe, Americus and Plains - the home of former President Jimmy Carter. His home is a modest ranch house and the old railroad station is a museum for his early campaigning. The area is rural, very poor and desolate. It leaves a northerner with a feeling of what the old South must have been like after the Civil War.

There were three groups of people affected by the Civil War and reconstruction in the South. Like my character, David Wexley, I too have inexplicable feelings about the South; an inexplicable attraction that is appealing, melancholy and conflictive. Part of it is my Scots-Irish heritage and its manifestations in the poor whites of the South. Part of it is my bond with, and love for, my friend Abraham and his strength of character and great heart. Most of it is the lessons of humanity and inhumanity so vividly taught there.

I wanted to write about the old verities. I chose the context I understand best to illustrate them. This historical fictional work has depicted our American tragedy, during the most powerful period of our history, surmounting our greatest challenge, with triumph over horrific circumstances affecting the lives of all our American people. In the end, the book is about hope. All of life comes to that conclusion and finality.

Influential References

Webb, James, *Born Fighting - How the Scots-Irish Shaped America*, New York: Broadway Books, 2004 - eISBN: 978-0-7679-2295-1, v3.0

Foner, Eric, *Reconstruction America's Unfinished Revolution, 1863-1877*, New York: Harper & Row, 1988 - ISBN: 978-0-06-093716-4

Stowe, Harriet Beecher, *Uncle Tom's Cabin or Life Among the Lowly*, University of Oxford Text Archive, 1852

Jakes, John, *North and South, Part I*, New York: Penguin Putnam, 1982 - ISBN: 0-451-20081-0

Cornwell, Bernard, *The Bloody Ground, The Nathaniel Starbuck Chronicles, Book Four, Battle of Antietam, 1862*, New York: Harper Collins, 1996 - ISBN: 0-06-093719-X

Shaara, Jeff, *The Last Full Measure*, New York: Ballantine Publishing, 1998 - ISBN: 0-345-40491-2

Shaara, Jeff, *A Blaze of Glory, A Novel of the Battle of Shiloh*, New York: Random House, 2012 - ISBN: 978-0-345-52735-6

Reasoner, James, *Shenandoah, Book 8, The Civil War Battle Series*, Nashville: Cumberland House, 2002 - ISBN: 1-58182-294-4

Hackman, Gene and Daniel Lenihan, *Escape From Andersonville, A Novel of the Civil War*, New York: St. Martin's Press, 2008 - ISBN-13: 978-0-312-36373-4, ISBN-10: 0-312-36373-7

MacDonald, John, *Great Battles of the Civil War*, New York: Chartwell Books, Inc., 2014 - ISBN: 10:0-7858-3095-2, ISBN: 13:978-0-7858-3095-5

Knauer, Kelly (editor/writer), *The Civil War - The Final Year*, New York: Time Books, 2014 forward by Jeff Shaara

Grahame-Smith, Seth, *Abraham Lincoln: Vampire Killer*, New York: Grand Central Publishing, 2010 - ISBN: 978-14555-1018-4

Faulkner, William, *Absalom, Absalom!*, New York: Random House, 1936 - ISBN 978-0-679-73218-1

The poetry and tender heart of Rod McKuen, the courage and fortitude of Nelson Mandela, the grit and forceful character of Theodore Roosevelt

Fictional Characters

The Protagonists-
> Josiah Ashford - slave and freedman, Savannah Oaks plantation
> David Wexley - northern Union soldier from Baltimore

The Antagonists-
> Marcus Taylor - Savannah Oaks plantation owner and slaveholder
> John Manford - Drish plantation overseer

Supporting Cast in order of appearance-
> Hendrick Taylor - Marcus's father
> Jane Taylor - Marcus's mother
> Marcy and Constance Taylor - Marcus's sisters
> Benjamin - Plantation overseer, Savannah Oaks

Ned - Slave carpenter, Savannah Oaks plantation

Rebecca Stanley Taylor - Marcus's wife, Charleston southern belle

William and Francis Stanley - Rebecca's brothers

Josena Taylor Ashford - Josiah's wife and a slave, Savannah Oaks and Drish plantations

Morgan Wexley - David's father

Geoff Braxton - Master carpenter, Union soldier from Baltimore

Patrick Allister - Union soldier from Massachusetts

Mary Custis Ashford - Josiah's 2nd wife

David Custis Ashford, Josena Custis Ashford - Josiah's children

Jeremiah Johnston - Drifter, Union soldier from Buffalo

Bill Wallis - Drifter, Union soldier from Buffalo

Jim and Lucy Culpepper - Freeborn Ohio farmers

Estelle Culpepper - Daughter

Historical Characters

The Union-

    U.S. Grant - Union Lieutenant General

    George McClellan, Union Major General

    Henry Halleck, Union Major General

    Ambrose Burnside, Union Major General

    William T. Sherman - Union Major General

    Philip H. (Little Phil) Sheridan - Union General

    George Meade, Union Major General

The Confederacy-

    Robert E. Lee - Confederate Brigadier General

    Thomas J. (Stonewall) Jackson - Confederate Lieutenant General

A.P. Hill - Confederate Major, Brigadier and Lieutenant
General

James Longstreet - Confederate Lieutenant General

P.G.T. Beauregard - Confederate General

J.E.B. (Beauty) Stuart - Confederate Major General

Albert Johnston - Confederate General

The Politicians-

Abraham Lincoln - U.S. President

John C. Calhoun - South Carolina U.S. House of
Representatives and U.S. Senator, U.S. Secretary of War,
U.S. Secretary of State, U.S. Vice President

John Crittenden - Kentucky Governor, U.S. House of
Representatives and U.S. Senator, U.S. Attorney General

Stephen Douglas - Illinois U.S. House of Representatives
and U.S. Senator

Henry Clay - Kentucky U.S. House of Representatives,
Speaker, U. .S. Secretary of   State

The Slaveholders-

John Drish - Owner Drish plantation near Tuscaloosa,
Alabama

Locations

Savannah, Georgia - place of Marcus Taylor's birth

Charleston, South Carolina - place of Rebecca Stanley's birth

Atlanta, Georgia - Confederate city destroyed by Sherman

Natchez, Mississippi - port near Savannah Oaks Plantation

Mobile, Alabama - Gulf port site of Union occupancy

Demopolis, Alabama - Freedmen's Bureau assistance center

Tuscaloosa, Alabama - John Drish Plantation

McComb, Mississippi - town developed near Savannah Oaks

Baltimore, Maryland - place of David Wexley's birth

Sharpsburg, Maryland - Battle of Antietam
The Wilderness, Virginia - Battle near Richmond

Richmond, Virginia - Capital of the Confederacy

Andersonville, Georgia - Prison camp for Union soldiers

Shiloh, Tennessee - Battle of Pittsburg Landing

Covington, Kentucky - city across Ohio river from Cincinnati

Cincinnati, Ohio - large city north of Ohio river

Hamilton, Ohio - small farm community near Cincinnati

Aspen, Colorado - silver mining town out west

Made in the USA
Middletown, DE
29 June 2015